Welfare and Social Security Programs

Other Books of Related Interest

Opposing Viewpoints Series
America's Great Divide
Capitalism
Poverty, Prosperity, and the Minimum Wage

At Issue Series
Food Security
Is America a Democracy or an Oligarchy?
Universal Health Care

Current Controversies Series
Are There Two Americas?
Homelessness and Street Crime
Learned Helplessness, Welfare, and the Poverty Cycle

> "Congress shall make no law … abridging the freedom of speech, or of the press."
>
> *First Amendment to the U.S. Constitution*

The basic foundation of our democracy is the First Amendment guarantee of freedom of expression. The Opposing Viewpoints series is dedicated to the concept of this basic freedom and the idea that it is more important to practice it than to enshrine it.

Welfare and Social Security Programs

Lisa Idzikowski, Book Editor

Published in 2024 by Greenhaven Publishing, LLC
2544 Clinton Street,
Buffalo NY 14224

Copyright © 2024 by Greenhaven Publishing, LLC

First Edition

All rights reserved. No part of this book may be reproduced in any form without permission in writing from the publisher, except by a reviewer.

Articles in Greenhaven Publishing anthologies are often edited for length to meet page requirements. In addition, original titles of these works are changed to clearly present the main thesis and to explicitly indicate the author's opinion. Every effort is made to ensure that Greenhaven Publishing accurately reflects the original intent of the authors. Every effort has been made to trace the owners of the copyrighted material.

Cover image: bbernard/Shutterstock.com

Library of Congress CataloginginPublication Data

Names: Idzikowski, Lisa, editor.
Title: Welfare and social security / edited by Lisa Idzikowski.
Description: First edition. | New York : Greenhaven Publishing,
 2024. | Series: Opposing viewpoints | Includes index.
Identifiers: ISBN 9781534509696 (pbk.) | ISBN 9781534509702 (library bound)
Subjects: LCSH: Public welfare--United States--Juvenile literature. | Social security--
 United States--Juvenile literature. | United States--Social policy--Juvenile literature.
Classification: LCC HV91.W466 2024 | DDC 362.5'5680973--dc23

Manufactured in the United States of America

Website: http://greenhavenpublishing.com

Contents

The Importance of Opposing Viewpoints	11
Introduction	14

Chapter 1: Have Welfare and Social Security Programs Improved Over Time?

Chapter Preface	18
1. There Are Many Misunderstandings About Americans Who Receive Government Aid *Joy Moses*	19
2. President Lyndon B. Johnson Declared War on Poverty *Lyndon B. Johnson*	29
3. President Biden's Decision to Overturn Welfare Reform Is Regressive *Matt Weidinger*	39
4. Modern Day Racism Prevents Those in Need from Getting Assistance *Alma Carten*	43
5. The War on Poverty Hasn't Been Won, but Government Aid Helps Americans Get By *Pam Fessler*	50
Periodical and Internet Sources Bibliography	55

Chapter 2: Should the Government Be Responsible for Welfare and Social Security Programs?

Chapter Preface	58
1. The Government Should Ensure Americans Have Health Coverage *Kristen Bialik*	59
2. Is the Myth of Welfare Dependency Valid? *Rema Hanna*	64

3. Many Americans Have Received Government Benefits 72
   Rich Morin, Paul Taylor, and Eileen Patten
4. Are There People Who Take Advantage of
   Public Assistance? 83
   Gene Demby
5. The Government Needs to Fix Corruption in State
   Social Service Programs 88
   Anna Wolfe
6. As a Society, We Should Be Able to Ask One Another
   for Help 97
   Melissa De Witte

Periodical and Internet Sources Bibliography 103

Chapter 3: Is the U.S.'s Social Safety Net Better than Other Countries'?

Chapter Preface 106

1. All Countries Must Enact Social Protection Networks 107
   The International Labor Organization
2. The United States Has a Poor Health Care System
   Compared to Other Countries 112
   Eric C. Schneider
3. There Are Various Reasons Why the United States Resists
   Universal Health Coverage 119
   Timothy Callaghan
4. France, Denmark, Norway, and Sweden Spend
   More than the United States on Social Programs 125
   David Squires and Chloe Anderson

Periodical and Internet Sources Bibliography 136

Chapter 4: What Is the Future of Welfare and Social Security?

Chapter Preface 139

1. Countries Need to Be Better Prepared for Crises
Like COVID **140**
John Power
2. Social Welfare Services Must Be Maintained for
the Good of the Country **144**
Nehal El-Hadi and Daniel Merino
3. The Future of Social Security Must Be Addressed Now **149**
Andrew Rettenmaier and Dennis W. Jansen
4. Welfare Can Pave the Way to More Equal Societies
and Less Conflict **155**
Patricia Justino

Periodical and Internet Sources Bibliography **160**

For Further Discussion **162**
Organizations to Contact **164**
Bibliography of Books **168**
Index **170**

The Importance of Opposing Viewpoints

Perhaps every generation experiences a period in time in which the populace seems especially polarized, starkly divided on the important issues of the day and gravitating toward the far ends of the political spectrum and away from a consensus-facilitating middle ground. The world that today's students are growing up in and that they will soon enter into as active and engaged citizens is deeply fragmented in just this way. Issues relating to terrorism, immigration, women's rights, minority rights, race relations, health care, taxation, wealth and poverty, the environment, policing, military intervention, the proper role of government—in some ways, perennial issues that are freshly and uniquely urgent and vital with each new generation—are currently roiling the world.

If we are to foster a knowledgeable, responsible, active, and engaged citizenry among today's youth, we must provide them with the intellectual, interpretive, and critical-thinking tools and experience necessary to make sense of the world around them and of the all-important debates and arguments that inform it. After all, the outcome of these debates will in large measure determine the future course, prospects, and outcomes of the world and its peoples, particularly its youth. If they are to become successful members of society and productive and informed citizens, students need to learn how to evaluate the strengths and weaknesses of someone else's arguments, how to sift fact from opinion and fallacy, and how to test the relative merits and validity of their own opinions against the known facts and the best possible available information. The landmark series Opposing Viewpoints has been providing students with just such critical-thinking skills and exposure to the debates surrounding society's most urgent contemporary issues for many years, and it continues to serve this essential role with undiminished commitment, care, and rigor.

The key to the series's success in achieving its goal of sharpening students' critical-thinking and analytic skills resides in its title—

Opposing Viewpoints. In every intriguing, compelling, and engaging volume of this series, readers are presented with the widest possible spectrum of distinct viewpoints, expert opinions, and informed argumentation and commentary, supplied by some of today's leading academics, thinkers, analysts, politicians, policy makers, economists, activists, change agents, and advocates. Every opinion and argument anthologized here is presented objectively and accorded respect. There is no editorializing in any introductory text or in the arrangement and order of the pieces. No piece is included as a "straw man," an easy ideological target for cheap point-scoring. As wide and inclusive a range of viewpoints as possible is offered, with no privileging of one particular political ideology or cultural perspective over another. It is left to each individual reader to evaluate the relative merits of each argument—as he or she sees it, and with the use of ever-growing critical-thinking skills—and grapple with his or her own assumptions, beliefs, and perspectives to determine how convincing or successful any given argument is and how the reader's own stance on the issue may be modified or altered in response to it.

This process is facilitated and supported by volume, chapter, and selection introductions that provide readers with the essential context they need to begin engaging with the spotlighted issues, with the debates surrounding them, and with their own perhaps shifting or nascent opinions on them. In addition, guided reading and discussion questions encourage readers to determine the authors' point of view and purpose, interrogate and analyze the various arguments and their rhetoric and structure, evaluate the arguments' strengths and weaknesses, test their claims against available facts and evidence, judge the validity of the reasoning, and bring into clearer, sharper focus the reader's own beliefs and conclusions and how they may differ from or align with those in the collection or those of their classmates.

Research has shown that reading comprehension skills improve dramatically when students are provided with compelling, intriguing, and relevant "discussable" texts. The subject matter of these collections could not be more compelling, intriguing, or urgently relevant to today's students and the world they are poised to inherit. The anthologized articles and the reading and discussion questions that are included with them also provide the basis for stimulating, lively, and passionate classroom debates. Students who are compelled to anticipate objections to their own argument and identify the flaws in those of an opponent read more carefully, think more critically, and steep themselves in relevant context, facts, and information more thoroughly. In short, using discussable text of the kind provided by every single volume in the Opposing Viewpoints series encourages close reading, facilitates reading comprehension, fosters research, strengthens critical thinking, and greatly enlivens and energizes classroom discussion and participation. The entire learning process is deepened, extended, and strengthened.

For all of these reasons, Opposing Viewpoints continues to be exactly the right resource at exactly the right time—when we most need to provide readers with the critical-thinking tools and skills that will not only serve them well in school but also in their careers and their daily lives as decision-making family members, community members, and citizens. This series encourages respectful engagement with and analysis of opposing viewpoints and fosters a resulting increase in the strength and rigor of one's own opinions and stances. As such, it helps make readers "future ready," and that readiness will pay rich dividends for the readers themselves, for the citizenry, for our society, and for the world at large.

Introduction

> *"Well-designed social protection measures are powerful tools for governments to reduce poverty and economic inequality and to meet their human rights obligations."*
>
> —*Human Rights Watch 2022*

Welfare and social security programs are not new. Before governmental programs began, extended family often took care of those unable to work or support themselves. Many changes happened over time in the United States that made this familial system unworkable. A large shift occurred when many people left rural areas and farming for life in big cities and better paying jobs. People began living longer which meant that many were unable to work in old age. The stock market crash of 1929 and the Great Depression that followed forever changed the United States. Then in the mid 1930s, President Franklin D. Roosevelt signed legislation that created the social safety nets of Social Security and welfare.

Social security, according to *Merriam-Webster,* is "the principle or practice of a program of public provision (as through social insurance or assistance) for the economic security and social welfare of the individual and his or her family." And welfare is defined as "aid in the form of money or necessities for people in need."

Not surprisingly, social safety net programs have had their supporters and critics. Some politicians and political parties rallied behind the idea of helping people in need. President Franklin Roosevelt said that "we can never insure 100 percent of the population against 100 percent of the hazards and vicissitudes of life, but we have tried to frame a law which will give some measure of protection to the average citizen and to his family against the loss of a job and against poverty-ridden old age." Others argued that assistance would make people lazy. Interestingly, some people at the time refused to accept help from the government out of shame for being perceived as poor and in need of assistance.

Through the years, many administrations made changes to the laws governing public assistance programs. In 1964, President Lyndon B. Johnson declared a war on poverty. At the time, nearly 20 percent of Americans were poor. Johnson considered it a failure for the country to have impoverished citizens and he enacted legislation to try to end poverty. President Richard M. Nixon also tried to conquer poverty. His solution was to promote stable families by encouraging people to get married. President Bill Clinton also tried his hand at relieving poverty. His efforts focused on moving people off public assistance and into stable jobs. It's important to note that despite these efforts there have always been people in need and it most likely will continue to be that way into the future. Look at one program alone, the Supplemental Nutrition Assistance Program (SNAP). It is informally known as food stamps, and in 2019 (the most recent data available), approximately 38 million people across the United States used this service so that they could feed themselves and their families.[1]

The issue of welfare, social security, and other public assistance programs is very complex. There have always been those who decry such programs and insist that the government should not be involved. And then of course there are others who claim that not enough is being done to help those in need. Interestingly, compared to many other developed countries around the world, the United States provides less help to its disadvantaged citizens. How is it possible that one of the richest nations on Earth struggles to meet the needs of underprivileged people? How the government can best assist these people in a sustainable way is up for debate. But one thing is very clear: social welfare programs are needed now and will continue to be necessary into the future. The elderly and retired, the disabled, injured, and sick, children, mothers, and many others across the population will need assistance at some time in their lives.

The complex debate surrounding the issue of social safety nets is explored in *Opposing Viewpoints: Welfare and Social Security Programs*, shedding light on this divisive and ongoing contemporary issue.

Notes

1. Lauren Hall and Catlin Nchako, "A Closer Look at Who Benefits from SNAP: State-by-State Fact Sheets," Center on Budget and Policy Priorities, February 13, 2023. https://www.cbpp.org/research/a-closer-look-at-who-benefits-from-snap-state-by-state-fact-sheets#Alabama.

CHAPTER 1

Have Welfare and Social Security Programs Improved Over Time?

Chapter Preface

Do people often think about the topic of Social Security or welfare? What are these programs, and do they impact every individual or every family in the United States? These programs are widespread in the United States, and there is a good chance that most families encounter them in one way or another.

One may wonder exactly who or what these programs impact. Are they only for people living in poverty? What about senior citizens, or people with disabilities? Does everyone qualify for benefits, or are they only for individuals who have worked or are working? Do the taxes taken out of a person's paycheck pay for these programs? There are many questions to consider about this wide-ranging topic. There are also many myths and outright misconceptions about it that have stayed alive in the public imagination.

The viewpoints in this chapter analyze, describe, and expand upon what Social Security and welfare are and the role they have played in American society since their initiation. The viewpoint authors provide definitions of this issue and answer questions relevant to the topic. What is government spending in reference to social welfare programs? Are governments responsible for citizens in need of assistance? What role does systemic racism play in this complex system? How have approaches to welfare and Social Security changed over time? Reading and thinking about the viewpoints in this chapter will provide a base of insight into these programs.

Viewpoint 1

> "*Recipients who benefit from the nation's major social insurance programs—Social Security, Medicare, and unemployment insurance . . . have paid into them, through payroll taxes taken out of their own paychecks and through contributions paid on their behalf by their employers.*"

There Are Many Misunderstandings About Americans Who Receive Government Aid

Joy Moses

In the following viewpoint Joy Moses asserts that most Americans who receive government benefits are not lazy people who do not want to work, as negative stereotypes often suggest. Moses contends that conservatives push erroneous ideas about government public assistance and the people who receive it. She outlines the types of public benefits and clears up misconceptions that give public benefit programs a bad reputation. There are many circumstances that can cause someone to be unable to work or find a job that pays enough to cover the cost of living, and these programs play an essential role in assisting people in those circumstances. Joy Moses is a senior policy analyst with the economic policy team at the Center for American Progress.

"The Facts About Americans Who Receive Public Benefits," by Joy Moses, Center for American Progress, December 16, 2011. Reprinted by permission.

As you read, consider the following questions:

1. What is common about many Americans receiving either Medicare or Social Security, according to Moses?
2. According to the author, what does the phrase "public benefits" mean to many?
3. Which two populations in the United States receive public benefits as stated in the viewpoint?

Gross misperceptions about who receives public benefits and for what purposes are leading the nation toward debates that distract from the real problems facing middle-class and low-income Americans. Most public benefits spending is for participants, largely senior citizens, who have paid for the services via a lifetime of work. This is far different from the picture painted by many conservatives of public benefits being for lazy poor people who do not want to work. These misperceptions put all public benefits programs at risk, including those that reach the middle class. They also derail benefits programs that specifically target people living in poverty and help them to join the middle class.

The facts about public benefits detailed in this issue brief help shape the real debate Americans should be engaged in—how to fund and shape public benefits programs that largely serve the middle class and those living in poverty for the long haul.

Fact: Most Americans Receiving Public Benefits Paid for Them

For many, the phrase "public benefits" implies money handed out to poor people—but that's not the case. Recipients who benefit from the nation's major social insurance programs—Social Security, Medicare, and unemployment insurance—include middle-class and low-income Americans. In 2010, 39 percent of households had at least one person participating in at least one of these programs. Within the fiscal year 2011 budget, those three programs accounted for an estimated 60 percent of the dollars going out to individuals.

Within these social insurance programs, most of the participants have paid into them, through payroll taxes taken out of their own paychecks and through contributions paid on their behalf by their employers. Like private life or property insurance, everyone makes regular contributions with the expectation that when a certain event occurs (in the case of public benefits, that event could be retirement, disability, or temporary job loss), they will be protected and able to collect benefits they have paid for.

Conservatives focus on how the costs of these programs have grown over the past several decades, but so too have the public's payments into them. Currently payments into social insurance programs represent an estimated 37 percent (or $807 billion) of federal receipts in 2011, compared to 17 percent (or $124 billion) in 1961 and 31 percent (or $455 billion) in 1981, including federal employees' payments into their retirement accounts (the historical numbers are adjusted for inflation).

These programs reflect what Americans value. Clearly our nation believes there should be programs that ensure senior citizens who work throughout their lives and contribute to these programs should have a minimum level of security and care safe from the ups and downs of the stock market. Social Security and Medicare account for 55 percent of federal benefits dollars. When we hear about how so many Americans are living off the government, this myth is often used to perpetuate a stereotype of poor adults unwilling to work. In fact, it reflects the many Americans who have paid into programs such as Social Security and Medicare and no longer work due to age and disability.

Fact: Most Public Benefits Targeting Low-Income Americans Are Not Paid in Cash

Only about 10 percent of all federal dollars devoted to public benefits programs for low-income Americans are paid in cash. And of that 10 percent, more than two out of every three dollars are for Social Security disability benefits for individuals who have demonstrated to the government that they have a disability that interferes with their ability to work. The remaining cash payments go to needy Americans under the Temporary Assistance for Needy Families program. Participation in this program is low due to changes made in the 1990s that promoted work and created a five-year lifetime limit on participation.

The bottom line: Conservative rhetoric that the federal government routinely hands out checks to people who are too lazy to work is grossly inaccurate. Today federal cash assistance programs primarily focus on those unable to work.

What's more, the noncash benefits programs are each targeted toward a singular basic need. The largest ones, Medicaid and the Supplemental Nutrition Assistance Program, are entitlements (meaning services are guaranteed to those who meet program criteria) targeting health care and food needs. Many Medicaid beneficiaries live in deep poverty, with 38 percent of participating children falling well below the current poverty line in many states. And low-income families receiving food stamps through the Supplemental Nutrition Assistance Program desperately need the additional help for food purchases. Case in point: Additional food assistance provided by the Recovery Act in 2010 kept 1 million people out of poverty.

Conservatives decry spending increases on these entitlement programs. Yet upswings in Americans falling into poverty through no fault of their own during certain periods such as the Great Recession of 2007-2009 as well as growing income inequality in the long term are at the root of more spending on basic public benefits programs. Moreover, most other forms of targeted, noncash benefits programs such as low-income housing and energy assistance as well as higher education assistance are not entitlements. Their funding, decided on a yearly basis, tends to help only a small portion of those who qualify.

Fact: Many Beneficiaries of Low-Income Public Benefits Programs Are Elderly and Disabled

As noted above, Social Security and Medicare account for much of our nation's spending on public benefits. But other programs not specifically designated for the elderly reach a significant number of them as well as Americans with disabilities. The biggest programs demonstrate this point. Among those Americans receiving food assistance under the Supplemental Nutrition Assistance Program, 36 percent of households have an elderly or disabled person. When it comes to Medicaid, in 2008, 65 percent of payments were for those 65 and over, blind, or disabled.

Fact: Investments in Programs that Offer a Hand up to Americans in Poverty Are Consistently Small

To minimize spending on poverty-related entitlement programs, we could let more people go hungry or deprive them of life-sustaining medical insurance—steps that some conservatives fully embrace. Republican members of Congress, for example, regularly proposed cuts to Medicaid and federal food assistance as a part of this year's deficit reduction efforts. Many of these efforts fortunately have been fruitless.

Alternatively, we could aggressively act to reduce poverty, which in turn would reduce the number of people in need of basic needs assistance. This would require a dramatic shift in priorities. Over the past 30 years, spending on education, training, employment, and social services remained a consistently small part of the overall federal budget, hovering around 3 percent. In fiscal year 2011, which closed at the end of September, it is estimated that spending on these programs amounted to a little more than $120 billion. By way of comparison, defense spending is more than six times that amount, at an estimated $768 billion in FY 2011.

The hard facts are that more federal money is being spent on basic-needs entitlements, while the share of spending going

---

President Johnson's "Great Society"

Vice President Lyndon B. Johnson became president automatically when President John F. Kennedy was assassinated. He wanted to create a "Great Society" and to end poverty and racial injustice.

The War on Poverty

Johnson called for an "all-out war on poverty." His vision of a Great Society included measures on:

- poverty
- civil rights
- transportation
- urban renewal
- the environment
- health care reform
- education reform

In November 1964, Johnson was elected president in his own right. The following anti-poverty programme measures were part of Johnson's attack on poverty:

- The 1964 Economic Opportunity Act allocated money to provide training, development and educational opportunities for the unemployed. It was hoped that this would help to break the cycle of poverty in deprived communities.
- The 1965 Housing and Urban Development Act was designed to combat the decline in city housing standards. The standards in housing had worsened with the increase in the number of people moving from cities to the *suburbs*. The act provided *federal* funds to cities for urban renewal and established minimum housing standards.

toward programs that would best reduce poverty (education, training, employment, and social services) have largely remained the same from one year to the next. In the real world this means that quality programs serving children, youth, students, and workers must water down their services and/or reach only a

Healthcare Reform

Supporters of *laissez-faire* and the American Medical Association had been powerful opponents of health care reform since the New Deal. However, Johnson was able to overcome their objections and pass two key measures under the 1965 Medicare and Medicaid Act.

- Medicare: This covered the cost of healthcare for the elderly if they qualified.
- Medicaid: This covered the cost of healthcare for people on low incomes and the unemployed.

Education

Johnson had been a teacher before he began his political career. He made education a key aspect of his war on poverty. Johnson believed that education offered a way out of poverty by providing children with more opportunities and improved standards.

- Operation Head Start: This was a programme intended to meet the needs of pre-school children from low-income families.
- 1965 Higher Education Act: This act increased funding to colleges and universities. It also created scholarships and provided low-interest loans to students.
- 1965 Elementary and Secondary Education Act: This provided major funding for education in school districts where the majority of students came from low-income families. This made education a federal responsibility. The funding was used to buy resources and for teachers' professional development. This act was one of the most comprehensive federal laws on education ever passed by Congress.

"America and the Great Society," BBC.

fraction of those people that stand to benefit. Because dramatic poverty reduction and growth in the middle class fails to occur, those needing help with basic needs such as food continues to grow.

What Needs to Be Done

Many Americans don't understand the basic facts about public benefits programs because conservatives so effectively peddle their myths. To combat these distortions, progressives not only need to present accurate information about these programs but also must focus more attention on issues that should be at the heart of our national conversation. This will help align good policy decisions with bedrock American values.

As noted above, current federal spending on public benefits is significantly directed toward those Americans who are retired or disabled and who often face subtle-yet-insidious workplace discrimination due to their age or disabilities. Further, when it comes to seniors, most have already completed a lifetime's worth of work and are simply drawing down on programs that they significantly paid into.

Simply put, elderly and disabled Americans should receive public support from the federal government. Can we agree that in America we should at least be providing these minimal resources for the elderly and disabled? Recent Census data suggest that seniors aren't living as well as official poverty numbers suggest due to out-of-pocket medical expenses and other factors. Should we be doing even more to assist seniors? The answer is yes.

This also means we need to support the social insurance programs such as Social Security and unemployment insurance that have served Americans well for decades. These programs aren't perfect but that is hardly an argument for destroying them. Experts at CAP [Center for American Progress] and elsewhere argue that we can find progressive ways of reforming Social

Security and unemployment insurance so that they better serve participants and the needs of our nation.

Similarly, we should be investing more in our children, our youth, and our young workers. Twenty-two percent of Americans under the age of 18 live in poverty, and young workers have the highest rates of unemployment—with lifelong implications for their earning potential. Yet federal funding for programs to give a leg up to our next generation of workers is dismally low. Federal student aid accounts for about 2 percent of the federal budget. And federal support for child care, which opens up better employment opportunities for young workers and has the potential to improve children's school readiness, accounts for only 0.2 percent of the federal budget.

The share of the federal budget spent on education, training, employment, and social services hasn't changed much over the past couple of decades. If we reduced poverty, we could reduce spending on basic-needs entitlements while having more citizens who are earning incomes that allow them to contribute more to our economy and contribute more tax revenue to our government.

Education, training, and employment services are needed to improve our nation's economic competitiveness, too. Our children and workers won't be able to properly compete with other nations with just 3 percent of the budget going to investments. For those Americans living in poverty, struggling to enter the middle class, federal spending should be devoted to programs that give them opportunities to prosper on their own. That means federal assistance with health insurance, food, housing, home energy, and education so these Americans can concentrate on opportunities to join the middle class.

Today's misplaced debate about how much to cut from federal benefits programs needs to become an honest debate about who receives public benefits and for what purposes so that we can retool benefits programs to better help all Americans, including those living in poverty, to have a piece of the American Dream. Federal programs that help reduce poverty and grow the middle class help our national economy and our nation remain strong and competitive. This is the debate we should be having today.

VIEWPOINT 2

> "On similar occasions in the past we have often been called upon to wage war against foreign enemies which threatened our freedom. Today we are asked to declare war on a domestic enemy which threatens the strength of our nation and the welfare of our people."

President Lyndon B. Johnson Declared War on Poverty

Lyndon B. Johnson

In the following viewpoint, Lyndon B. Johnson, who was the President of the United States from 1963 to 1969, expresses his views on poverty in the United States and the ways it can be combatted. The viewpoint is a transcript of a speech President Johnson gave to Congress in 1964 describing his plan for fighting poverty and encouraging them to pass the Economic Opportunity Act of 1964, which focused on providing job training, loans for small business, and adult education opportunities to fight unemployment. Johnson contends that America can and must win a war against poverty. Lyndon Baines Johnson was the 36th president of the United States.

"Special Message to the Congress Proposing a Nationwide War on the Sources of Poverty," by Lyndon B. Johnson, March 16, 1964, The American Presidency Project, https://www.presidency.ucsb.edu/documents/special-message-the-congress-proposing-nationwide-war-the-sources-poverty. Reprinted by permission.

Welfare and Social Security Programs

As you read, consider the following questions:

1. What is America's goal, according to President Johnson?
2. What was the name of Johnson's plan to rid the United States of poverty?
3. What special program did Johnson want for young people in the United States at this time in history?

To the Congress of the United States:

We are citizens of the richest and most fortunate nation in the history of the world.

One hundred and eighty years ago we were a small country struggling for survival on the margin of a hostile land.

Today we have established a civilization of free men which spans an entire continent.

With the growth of our country has come opportunity for our people—opportunity to educate our children, to use our energies in productive work, to increase our leisure—opportunity for almost every American to hope that through work and talent he could create a better life for himself and his family.

The path forward has not been an easy one.

But we have never lost sight of our goal: an America in which every citizen shares all the opportunities of his society, in which every man has a chance to advance his welfare to the limit of his capacities.

We have come a long way toward this goal.

We still have a long way to go.

The distance which remains is the measure of the great unfinished work of our society.

To finish that work I have called for a national war on poverty. Our objective: total victory.

There are millions of Americans—one fifth of our people—who have not shared in the abundance which has been granted to most of us, and on whom the gates of opportunity have been closed.

What does this poverty mean to those who endure it?

It means a daily struggle to secure the necessities for even a meager existence. It means that the abundance, the comforts, the opportunities they see all around them are beyond their grasp.

Worst of all, it means hopelessness for the young.

The young man or woman who grows up without a decent education, in a broken home, in a hostile and squalid environment, in ill health or in the face of racial injustice—that young man or woman is often trapped in a life of poverty.

He does not have the skills demanded by a complex society. He does not know how to acquire those skills. He faces a mounting sense of despair which drains initiative and ambition and energy.

Our tax cut will create millions of new jobs—new exits from poverty.

But we must also strike down all the barriers which keep many from using those exits.

The war on poverty is not a struggle simply to support people, to make them dependent on the generosity of others.

It is a struggle to give people a chance.

It is an effort to allow them to develop and use their capacities, as we have been allowed to develop and use ours, so that they can share, as others share, in the promise of this nation.

We do this, first of all, because it is right that we should.

From the establishment of public education and land grant colleges through agricultural extension and encouragement to industry, we have pursued the goal of a nation with full and increasing opportunities for all its citizens.

The war on poverty is a further step in that pursuit.

We do it also because helping some will increase the prosperity of all.

Our fight against poverty will be an investment in the most valuable of our resources—the skills and strength of our people.

And in the future, as in the past, this investment will return its cost many fold to our entire economy.

Welfare and Social Security Programs

If we can raise the annual earnings of 10 million among the poor by only $1,000 we will have added 14 billion dollars a year to our national output. In addition we can make important reductions in public assistance payments which now cost us 4 billion dollars a year, and in the large costs of fighting crime and delinquency, disease and hunger.

This is only part of the story.

Our history has proved that each time we broaden the base of abundance, giving more people the chance to produce and consume, we create new industry, higher production, increased earnings and better income for all.

Giving new opportunity to those who have little will enrich the lives of all the rest.

Because it is right, because it is wise, and because, for the first time in our history, it is possible to conquer poverty, I submit, for the consideration of the Congress and the country, the Economic Opportunity Act of 1964.

The Act does not merely expand old programs or improve what is already being done.

It charts a new course.

It strikes at the causes, not just the consequences of poverty.

It can be a milestone in our 180-year search for a better life for our people.

This Act provides five basic opportunities.

It will give almost half a million underprivileged young Americans the opportunity to develop skills, continue education, and find useful work.

It will give every American community the opportunity to develop a comprehensive plan to fight its own poverty—and help them to carry out their plans.

It will give dedicated Americans the opportunity to enlist as volunteers in the war against poverty.

It will give many workers and farmers the opportunity to break through particular barriers which bar their escape from poverty.

It will give the entire nation the opportunity for a concerted attack on poverty through the establishment, under my direction, of the Office of Economic Opportunity, a national headquarters for the war against poverty.

This is how we propose to create these opportunities.

First we will give high priority to helping young Americans who lack skills, who have not completed their education or who cannot complete it because they are too poor.

The years of high school and college age are the most critical stage of a young person's life. If they are not helped then, many will be condemned to a life of poverty which they, in turn, will pass on to their children.

I therefore recommend the creation of a Job Corps, a Work-Training Program, and a Work Study Program.

A new national Job Corps will build toward an enlistment of 100,000 young men. They will be drawn from those whose background, health and education make them least fit for useful work.

Those who volunteer will enter more than 100 Camps and Centers around the country.

Half of these young men will work, in the first year, on special conservation projects to give them education, useful work experience and to enrich the natural resources of the country.

Half of these young men will receive, in the first year, a blend of training, basic education and work experience in Job Training Centers.

These are not simply camps for the underprivileged. They are new educational institutions, comparable in innovation to the land grant colleges. Those who enter them will emerge better qualified to play a productive role in American society.

A new national Work-Training Program operated by the Department of Labor will provide work and training for 200,000 American men and women between the ages of 16 and 21. This will be developed through state and local governments and non-profit agencies.

Welfare and Social Security Programs

Hundreds of thousands of young Americans badly need the experience, the income, and the sense of purpose which useful full or part-time work can bring. For them such work may mean the difference between finishing school or dropping out. Vital community activities from hospitals and playgrounds to libraries and settlement houses are suffering because there are not enough people to staff them.

We are simply bringing these needs together.

A new national Work-Study Program operated by the Department of Health, Education, and Welfare will provide federal funds for part-time jobs for 140,000 young Americans who do not go to college because they cannot afford it.

There is no more senseless waste than the waste of the brainpower and skill of those who are kept from college by economic circumstance. Under this program they will, in a great American tradition, be able to work their way through school.

They and the country will be richer for it.

Second, through a new Community Action Program we intend to strike at poverty at its source—in the streets of our cities and on the farms of our countryside among the very young and the impoverished old.

This program asks men and women throughout the country to prepare long-range plans for the attack on poverty in their own local communities.

These are not plans prepared in Washington and imposed upon hundreds of different situations.

They are based on the fact that local citizens best understand their own problems, and know best how to deal with those problems.

These plans will be local plans striking at the many unfilled needs which underlie poverty in each community, not just one or two. Their components and emphasis will differ as needs differ.

These plans will be local plans calling upon all the resources available to the community-federal and state, local and private, human and material.

And when these plans are approved by the Office of Economic Opportunity, the federal government will finance up to 9070 of the additional cost for the first two years.

The most enduring strength of our nation is the huge reservoir of talent, initiative and leadership which exists at every level of our society.

Through the Community Action Program we call upon this, our greatest strength, to overcome our greatest weakness.

Third, I ask for the authority to recruit and train skilled volunteers for the war against poverty.

Thousands of Americans have volunteered to serve the needs of other lands.

Thousands more want the chance to serve the needs of their own land.

They should have that chance.

Among older people who have retired, as well as among the young, among women as well as men, there are many Americans who are ready to enlist in our war against poverty.

They have skills and dedication. They are badly needed.

If the State requests them, if the community needs and will use them, we will recruit and train them and give them the chance to serve.

Fourth, we intend to create new opportunities for certain hard-hit groups to break out of the pattern of poverty.

Through a new program of loans and guarantees we can provide incentives to those who will employ the unemployed.

Through programs of work and retraining for unemployed fathers and mothers we can help them support their families in dignity while preparing themselves for new work.

Through funds to purchase needed land, organize cooperatives, and create new and adequate family farms we can help those whose life on the land has been a struggle without hope.

Welfare and Social Security Programs

Fifth, I do not intend that the war against poverty become a series of uncoordinated and unrelated efforts—that it perish for lack of leadership and direction.

Therefore this bill creates, in the Executive Office of the President, a new Office of Economic Opportunity. Its director will be my personal chief of staff for the war against poverty. I intend to appoint Sargent Shriver to this post.

He will be directly responsible for these new programs. He will work with and through existing agencies of the government.

This program—the Economic Opportunity Act—is the foundation of our war against poverty. But it does not stand alone.

For the past three years this government has advanced a number of new proposals which strike at important areas of need and distress.

I ask the Congress to extend those which are already in action, and to establish those which have already been proposed.

There are programs to help badly distressed areas such as the Area Redevelopment Act, and the legislation now being prepared to help Appalachia.

There are programs to help those without training find a place in today's complex society—such as the Manpower Development Training Act and the Vocational Education Act for youth.

There are programs to protect those who are specially vulnerable to the ravages of poverty—hospital insurance for the elderly, protection for migrant farm workers, a food stamp program for the needy, coverage for millions not now protected by a minimum wage, new and expanded unemployment benefits for men out of work, a Housing and Community Development bill for those seeking decent homes.

Finally there are programs which help the entire country, such as aid to education which, by raising the quality of schooling available to every American child, will give a new chance for knowledge to the children of the poor.

I ask immediate action on all these programs.

What you are being asked to consider is not a simple or an easy program. But poverty is not a simple or an easy enemy.

It cannot be driven from the land by a single attack on a single front. Were this so we would have conquered poverty long ago.

Nor can it be conquered by government alone.

For decades American labor and American business, private institutions and private individuals have been engaged in strengthening our economy and offering new opportunity to those in need.

We need their help, their support, and their full participation.

Through this program we offer new incentives and new opportunities for cooperation, so that all the energy of our nation, not merely the efforts of government, can be brought to bear on our common enemy.

Today, for the first time in our history, we have the power to strike away the barriers [p.380] to full participation in our society. Having the power, we have the duty.

The Congress is charged by the Constitution to "provide . . . for the general welfare of the United States." Our present abundance is a measure of its success in fulfilling that duty. Now Congress is being asked to extend that welfare to all our people.

The president of the United States is president of all the people in every section of the country. But this office also holds a special responsibility to the distressed and disinherited, the hungry and the hopeless of this abundant nation.

It is in pursuit of that special responsibility that I submit this message to you today.

The new program I propose is within our means. Its cost of 970 million dollars is 1 percent of our national budget—and every dollar I am requesting for this program is already included in the budget I sent to Congress in January.

But we cannot measure its importance by its cost.

For it charts an entirely new course of hope for our people.

Welfare and Social Security Programs

We are fully aware that this program will not eliminate all the poverty in America in a few months or a few years. Poverty is deeply rooted and its causes are many.

But this program will show the way to new opportunities for millions of our fellow citizens.

It will provide a lever with which we can begin to open the door to our prosperity for those who have been kept outside.

It will also give us the chance to test our weapons, to try our energy and ideas and imagination for the many battles yet to come. As conditions change, and as experience illuminates our difficulties, we will be prepared to modify our strategy.

And this program is much more than a beginning.

Rather it is a commitment. It is a total commitment by this president, and this Congress, and this nation, to pursue victory over the most ancient of mankind's enemies.

On many historic occasions the president has requested from Congress the authority to move against forces which were endangering the well-being of our country. This is such an occasion.

On similar occasions in the past we have often been called upon to wage war against foreign enemies which threatened our freedom. Today we are asked to declare war on a domestic enemy which threatens the strength of our nation and the welfare of our people.

If we now move forward against this enemy—if we can bring to the challenges of peace the same determination and strength which has brought us victory in war—then this day and this Congress will have won a secure and honorable place in the history of the nation, and the enduring gratitude of generations of Americans yet to come.

VIEWPOINT 3

> "*Especially if made permanent, partisan policies subsidizing non-work turn back the clock to what came before—when as Bill Clinton put it, welfare without work was an impoverished 'way of life' for too many American families.*"

President Biden's Decision to Overturn Welfare Reform Is Regressive

Matt Weidinger

In the following viewpoint Matt Weidinger analyzes and compares welfare reform from the laws passed by former President Bill Clinton and President Joe Biden. Weidinger contends that there are great differences in the welfare reform policies of President Biden compared to former President Clinton's. He claims that while Clinton's program focused on getting Americans jobs and off welfare, during the COVID pandemic, Biden shifted the focus to providing benefits to nonworking adults, especially in the form of child tax credits and food stamps. Weidinger considers it unwise to subsidize programs that are not focused on helping Americans find gainful employment. Matt Weidinger is a senior fellow and Rowe Scholar in opportunity and mobility studies at the American Enterprise Institute. His work focuses on many aspects of disability, welfare, and insurance.

"Turning Back the Clock on Welfare Reform," by Matt Weidinger, American Enterprise Institute, August 23, 2021. Reprinted by permission.

Welfare and Social Security Programs

As you read, consider the following questions:

1. According to the viewpoint, what did Bill Clinton's welfare reform require parents to do in order to receive benefits?
2. What happened as a result of the welfare reform, according to Weidinger?
3. As reported by the author, how has President Biden changed welfare reform policies?

This week marks the 25th anniversary of the 1996 welfare reform law. Crafted by congressional Republicans, that legislation was approved by large bipartisan majorities before being signed into law by President Bill Clinton. It marked the end of a former welfare program providing limitless monthly checks to non-working parents and equally limitless federal funds to cover the cost. In its place, a new program required benefits to be time-limited, expected parents to work or train for them, capped federal funds, and held states accountable for more work, less dependence, or both.

Opponents predicted disaster. The *New York Times* opined "This is not reform, it is punishment....The effect on cities will be devastating." The late Sen. Daniel Moynihan (D-NY) predicted children "sleeping on grates" in a dystopian Grate Society. Future Speaker Nancy Pelosi (D-CA) ventured "The Republican welfare reform proposal will make the problems of poverty and dependence much worse because it refuses to make work the cornerstone of welfare reform."

They were wrong.

After reform, welfare caseloads plummeted as millions of mothers left or stayed off the welfare rolls in favor of work. In just the five years after August 1996, the number of families on welfare dropped over 50 percent. Aided by a strong economy, the share of never-married mothers (the group most likely to go on welfare) who worked rose almost 40 percent over the four-year period beginning in 1996.

Child support grew and additional funds for childcare, extended health insurance, and tax credits that rewarded work all made going to work pay better than staying on welfare. As a result, earnings rose sharply while poverty plunged.

As the Congressional Budget Office noted in 2007, "Between 1991 and 2005, household earnings doubled (on average) in female-headed low-income households," with the change "driven by a large increase in earnings during the late 1990s." As household incomes swelled, poverty fell sharply—instead of rising as opponents predicted. For example, the rate and number of African American children in poverty reached record lows in 2001. By 2002, even the *New York Times* admitted "Welfare reform has been an obvious success."

While further reforms are overdue, most of those early gains endured in the years since. For example, the official child poverty rate in 2019 was 30 percent below the 1996 level—even without counting increases in food stamps and tax benefits promoting work. As AEI [American Enterprise Institute] president Robert Doar recently noted, if you count all taxpayer assistance, the "consumption" child poverty rate fell to just 3.7 percent in 2018, or by over 70 percent compared with the 1996 level.

But liberals are now using the pandemic as cover to roll back that work-based progress. President Biden in March signed a massive pandemic relief bill that effectively overturns welfare reform by reviving monthly government checks for low-income parents who don't work. It does so by converting the child tax credit—previously payable only to working parents—into bigger checks for even those who don't work at all.

That policy is in place for 2021, and in July, monthly federal checks worth up to $300 per child started flowing to 39 million households, including many headed by nonworking adults never before eligible for such "child tax credits." As one headline concisely put it "Goodbye, Clinton welfare reform. Hello, child tax credit." Supporters want to make this temporary policy permanent, but are expected to include only a brief extension in their massive spending bill this fall—because they lack offsets for the $1.6 trillion cost in the first decade alone.

Meanwhile the Biden administration just announced record increases in food stamp benefits for 42 million recipients. Approved without legislation, the increases total $20 billion per year—or more than the federal government spends on its share of the welfare program created in 1996. As AEI's Angela Rachidi notes, the result is a single parent with three children can now collect over $20,000 in annual food stamp and "child tax credit" benefits without working. That's the equivalent of a full-time job paying $10 per hour, without counting housing, energy, health, unemployment, disability, and other benefits the family might also collect without working.

The 1996 welfare reforms reflected a bipartisan sea change in the direction of promoting work instead of welfare as a solution to poverty. But the old Ronald Reagan adage remains true: If you want more of something, subsidize it. Especially if made permanent, partisan policies subsidizing non-work turn back the clock to what came before—when as Bill Clinton put it, welfare without work was an impoverished "way of life" for too many American families.

VIEWPOINT 4

> "U.S. welfare policy is, arguably, as much a reflection of its economic policies as it is of the nation's troublesome history of racism."

Modern Day Racism Prevents Those in Need from Getting Assistance

Alma Carten

In the following viewpoint Alma Carten argues that racism is deeply rooted in the fabric of the United States and is a major reason for the poverty of Black Americans. Furthermore, it has played a major role in shaping welfare policy. Carten outlines the history and progression of welfare and welfare reform measures. Widespread racial discrimination in workplaces caused Black Americans to have fewer job opportunities, which prevented them from benefitting from work-based social insurance programs. As workplace discrimination started to decrease, more Black Americans became eligible for these programs, contributing to the myth of the "Welfare Queen" popularized by former President Reagan. Alma Carten is an associate professor of social work at New York University. Dr. Carten's professional interests focus on child welfare.

"How racism has shaped welfare policy in America since 1935," by Alma Carten, The Conversation, August 22, 2016. https://theconversation.com/how-racism-has-shaped-welfare-policy-in-america-since-1935-63574. Licensed under CC-BY ND 4.0 International.

Welfare and Social Security Programs

As you read, consider the following questions:

1. As stated in the viewpoint, which population of American children are the most impoverished?
2. According to Carten, which two U.S. presidents reduced welfare?
3. Which bill replaced the Aid to Families of Dependent Children (AFDC) program, according to the author?

A recent UNICEF report found that the United States ranked 34th on the list of 35 developed countries surveyed on the well-being of children. According to the Pew Institute, children under the age of 18 are the most impoverished age population of Americans, and African-American children are almost four times as likely as white children to be in poverty.

These findings are alarming, not least because they come on the 20th anniversary of President [Bill] Clinton's promise to "end welfare as we know it" with his signing into law, on Aug. 23, 1996, the Personal Responsibility and Work Opportunity Reconciliation Act (P.L. 104-193).

It is true that the data show the number of families receiving cash assistance fell from 12.3 million in 1996 to current levels of 4.1 million as reported by The *New York Times*. But it is also true that child poverty rates for Black children remain stubbornly high in the United States.

My research indicates that this didn't happen by chance. In a recent book, I examine social welfare policy developments in the United States over a 50-year period from the New Deal to the 1996 reforms. Findings reveal that U.S. welfare policies have, from their very inception, been discriminatory.

Blemished by a History of Discrimination

It was the 1935 Social Security Act, introduced by the Franklin Roosevelt administration, that first committed the United States to the safety net philosophy.

From the beginning, the policy had two tiers that intended to protect families from loss of income.

On one level were the contributory social insurance programs that provided income support to the surviving dependents of workers in the event of their death or incapacitation and Social Security for retired older Americans.

The second tier was made up of means-tested public assistance programs that included what was originally called the "Aid to Dependent Children" program and was subsequently renamed the Aid to Families with Dependent Children in the 1962 Public Welfare Amendments to the SSA under the Kennedy administration.

The optimistic vision of the architects of the ADC program was that it would die "a natural death" with the rising quality of life in the country as a whole, resulting in more families becoming eligible for the work-related social insurance programs.

But this scenario was problematic for Black Americans because of pervasive racial discrimination in employment in the decades of the 1930s and 1940s. During these decades, Blacks typically worked in menial jobs. Not tied to the formal workforce, they were paid in cash and "off the books," making them ineligible for social insurance programs that called for contributions through payroll taxes from both employers and employees.

Nor did Blacks fare much better under ADC during these years.

The ADC was an extension of the state-operated mothers' pension programs, where white widows were the primary beneficiaries. The criteria for eligibility and need were state-determined, so Blacks continued to be barred from full participation because the country operated under the "separate but equal" doctrine adopted by the Supreme Court in 1896.

Jim Crow laws and the separate but equal doctrine resulted in the creation of a two-track service delivery system in both law and custom, one for whites and one for Blacks that were anything but equal.

Developments in the 1950s and '60s further disadvantaged Black families.

This happened when states stepped up efforts to reduce ADC enrollment and costs. As I examined in my book, residency requirements were proposed so as to bar Blacks migrating from the South to qualify for the program. New York City's "man in the house rule" required welfare workers to make unannounced visits to determine if fathers were living in the home—if evidence of a male presence was found, cases were closed and welfare checks discontinued.

Always an Unpopular Program

Because of the strong American work ethic, and preference for a "hand up" versus a "hand-out," the means-tested, cash assistance programs for poor families—and especially ADC renamed AFDC—have never been popular among Americans. As FDR himself said in his 1935 State of the Union address to Congress, "the government must and shall quit this business of relief."

As the quality of life did indeed improve for whites, the number of white widows and their children on the AFDC rolls declined. At the same time, the easing of racial discrimination widened eligibility to more Blacks, increasing the number of never-married women of color and their children who were born out of wedlock.

One point, however, to note here is that there has always been a public misconception about race and welfare. It is true that over the years Blacks became disproportionately represented. But given that whites constitute a majority of the population, numerically they have always been the largest users of the AFDC program.

Holes in the Safety Net

The retreat from the safety net philosophy can be dated to the presidencies of Richard Nixon and Ronald Reagan.

On the one hand, politicians wanted to reduce the cost of welfare. Under Reagan policies of New Federalism, social welfare expenditures were capped and responsibility for programs for poor families given back to states.

On the other hand, the demographic shift in the welfare rolls exacerbated the politics around welfare and racialized the debate.

Ronald Reagan's "Welfare Queen" narrative only reinforced existing white stereotypes about Blacks:

> *There's a woman in Chicago. She has 80 names, 30 addressees, 12 Social Security cards and is collecting veterans' benefits on four nonexistent deceased husbands. She's got Medicaid, is getting food stamps and welfare under each of her names. Her tax-free cash income alone is over $150,000.*

Reagan's assertions that the homeless were living on the streets by choice played to conventional wisdom about the causes of poverty, blamed poor people for their own misfortune and helped disparage government programs to help the poor.

The 1990s Gear Change

By the late 1990s efforts of reforms targeting the AFDC program shifted to more nuanced forms of racism with claims that the program encouraged out-of-wedlock births, irresponsible fatherhood and intergenerational dependency.

The political context for the 1996 reforms, then, was fueled by racist undertones that played into public angst about rising taxes and the national debt that were attributed to the high payout of welfare checks to people who were not carrying their own weight.

This emotionally charged environment distorted the poverty debate, and paved the way for a reform bill that many saw as excessively punitive in its harsh treatment of poor families.

Although credited to the Clinton administration, the blueprint for the 1996 welfare reform bill was crafted by a caucus of conservative Republicans led by Newt Gingrich as part of the Contract with America during the 1994 congressional election campaign.

Twice President Clinton vetoed the welfare reform bill sent to him by the GOP-dominated Congress. The third time he signed, creating much controversy, including the resignation of his own adviser on welfare reform, the leading scholar on poverty David Ellwood.

The new bill replaced the AFDC program with Temporary Assistance to Needy Families (TANF). Stricter work requirements required single mothers to find work within two years of receiving benefits. A five-year lifetime limit was imposed for receiving benefits. To reinforce traditional family values, a core principle of the Republican Party, teenage mothers were to be prohibited benefits, and fathers who were delinquent in child support payments were threatened with imprisonment. States were banned from using federally funded TANF for certain groups of immigrants and restrictions were placed on their eligibility to Medicaid, food stamps and Supplementary Social Security Income (SSI).

The Impact

Despite many bleak predictions, favorable outcomes were reported on the 10th anniversary of the bill's signing. Welfare rolls had declined. Mothers had moved from welfare to work and children had benefited psychologically from having an employed parent.

However, the volume of research generated at the 10-year benchmark has not been matched, in my observation, by that produced in years leading up to the 20-year anniversary.

More research in particular is needed to understand what is happening with families who have left welfare rolls because of passing the five-year lifetime limit for receiving benefits but have not sustained a foothold in an ever-increasing specialized workforce.

Disentangling Intertwined Effects of Racism and Poverty

U.S. welfare policy is, arguably, as much a reflection of its economic policies as it is of the nation's troublesome history of racism.

In the words of President [Barack] Obama, racism is a part of America's DNA and history. Similarly, the notion that anyone who is willing to work hard can be rich is just as much a part of that

DNA. Both have played an equal role in constraining adequate policy development for poor families and have been especially harmful to poor Black families.

Racism has left an indelible mark on American institutions. In particular, it influences how we understand the causes of poverty and how we develop solutions for ending it.

Indeed, with the continual unraveling of the safety net, the 20th anniversary of welfare reforms can be an impetus for taking a closer look at how racism has shaped welfare policy in the United States and to what extent it accounts for the persistently high poverty rates for Black children.

VIEWPOINT 5

> "Somebody asked me one time about the war on poverty, and I said, 'Well, it really wasn't a war—it was more of a skirmish.' And we need to declare war on poverty again."

The War on Poverty Hasn't Been Won, but Government Aid Helps Americans Get By

Pam Fessler

In this viewpoint Pam Fessler reports on life in Martin County, Kentucky, which former President Lyndon Johnson used as the face of poverty for his "war on poverty." But despite the government aid programs that Johnson helped put into place—and the various other aid programs that have been enacted since—Martin County is still impoverished. In some ways, things have improved in the county, as the hospitals, schools, and public infrastructure like roads are better than they used to be. Nonetheless, poverty rates and unemployment rates remain high. Many residents count on food stamps, energy assistance, and Supplemental Security Income to get by. In order to move out of poverty, residents believe the focus needs to shift to creating more job opportunities. Pam Fessler is a former correspondent for NPR News who focused on voting and poverty.

©2014 National Public Radio, Inc. NPR news report "Kentucky County That Gave War On Poverty A Face Still Struggles" by Pam Fessler was originally published on npr.org on January 8, 2014, and is used with the permission of NPR. Any unauthorized duplication is strictly prohibited.

Have Welfare and Social Security Programs Improved Over Time?

As you read, consider the following questions:

1. What was the poverty rate of Martin County when President Johnson visited in 1964?
2. What was the poverty rate of Martin County at the time this viewpoint was published?
3. According to this viewpoint, how do many Martin County residents feel about the government aid being provided?

People in the isolated hills of Martin County, Ky., rarely saw outsiders, let alone a president. So when President Lyndon Johnson visited in 1964 to generate support for his proposed war on poverty, it was a big deal.

Lee Mueller, a young newspaper reporter at the time, recalls the crowds in downtown Inez, Ky., the county seat, waiting for the presidential party to arrive at an abandoned miniature golf course.

"It was just like a hayfield full of long grass. It looked like helicopters landing in Vietnam or something when they came over the ridge," he says.

Mueller says the locals didn't know their role in this new, domestic war. For the White House, though, coming to Martin County gave poverty a face—and a name.

"In this south-central mountain country, over a third of the population is faced with chronic unemployment," says a government film on Johnson's visit. "Typical of this group is Tom Fletcher, his wife and eight children. Fletcher, an unemployed sawmill operator, earned only $400 last year and has been able to find little employment in the last two years."

At the time, the poverty rate in this coal-mining area was more than 60 percent. Johnson visited the Fletchers on the porch of their home—a small wooden structure with fake brick siding. Photographers took what would become one of the iconic images of the war on poverty: the president crouched down, chatting with Tom Fletcher about the lack of jobs.

Welfare and Social Security Programs

Fast-forward 50 years. The Fletcher cabin still stands along a windy road about 5 miles outside town. It now has wood siding and is painted orange. There's a metal fence with a "no trespassing" sign to keep out strangers. There are lots of small houses and trailers along this road, but also some new, bigger homes that could be found in any American suburb.

Today, the roads here are well-paved. People say the schools and hospitals are much better than they used to be. Still, Martin County remains one of the poorest counties in the country. Its poverty rate is 35 percent, more than twice the national average. Unemployment remains high. Only 9 percent of the adults have a college degree.

"I Would Be Homeless"

Much of the poverty today is tucked between the mountains in what are called "the hollers." That's where Norma Moore lives with her 8-year-old grandson, Brayden. She says his parents didn't want him. He was born with a rare blood disease and is severely disabled. "And they said he was dying, and then at 4 months I got him, and I've had him ever since," Moore says.

Brayden doesn't walk or talk. He's in constant motion, rolling on the floor of their double-wide trailer home, bumping into walls and doors.

There's no question that Moore's life is incredibly stressful. She says she gets by on her faith. But here's where the war on poverty has also made a big difference: Today, she gets food stamps and energy assistance to heat her home—programs with roots in Johnson's anti-poverty initiatives—as well as Supplemental Security Income (SSI) for her grandson.

Moore shakes her head thinking about life without the help. "I would be homeless. I would be the one living on the street if it wasn't for that," she says. She looks down at her grandson on the floor. "He would probably be in a home somewhere."

Today, many people here rely on government aid. In fact, it's the largest source of income in Martin County. People say it has helped to reduce hunger, improve health care and give young families a boost, especially at a time when coal-mining jobs are disappearing by the hundreds.

Head Start is one of the signature programs of the war on poverty—helping low- and moderate-income children get ready for school. Budget cuts are always a concern. Some of the county's children get their only hot meals of the day at school.

Delsie Fletcher helps Head Start parents in Martin County with services, such as getting their high school diplomas. And yes, Delsie is one of *those* Fletchers, married to one of the children who stood on the porch with President Johnson.

So has the war on poverty helped her husband's family? Turns out, along with the famous photo, it's a sore topic.

"They don't like to talk about it, because they don't want to be known as the poorest family in Martin County," she says.

And she says they probably weren't. Most of the Fletchers have done OK for themselves. Still, it hasn't been easy. Her husband had some of his toes cut off when he worked in the sawmills, and now he's on disability. Work around here can be tough—and dangerous—which is why coal-mining jobs pay so well. But now they're scarce, and there's nothing to replace them. People are struggling to adjust.

"I Call It Abusing the System"

Thomas Vinson, a Martin County resident for 41 years, used to work in the coal fields, but he is currently unemployed. Vinson says he has a big house payment and three sons to raise. Times are tough, he says, but "we are making it."

One reason is that Vinson's wife got a job at a gear factory through a federally funded program to help unemployed miners. Vinson is grateful for the short-term help but worried about his future. In the big picture, he's disappointed in the war on poverty. He says he sees too many people around here just collecting checks.

"They call it poverty, but I call it abusing the system. Like, if you're going to file for SSI, you go in there and say the right things, you'll come out of there with a check," he says.

His feelings are widespread around here: What good are all these government programs if they don't get you a job?

Mike Howell runs the Big Sandy Area Community Action Program where the Vinsons went for help. The program is a direct result of the war on poverty. Howell agrees that the war has yet to achieve its goals, but says the reason is a lack of support. The burst of enthusiasm after President Johnson's visit has waned, he says. Every year, his program has to fight for funds.

"We've kind of let poverty go to the side," says Howell. "It's still way too high. Somebody asked me one time about the war on poverty, and I said, 'Well, it really wasn't a war—it was more of a skirmish.' And we need to declare war on poverty again."

Periodical and Internet Sources Bibliography

The following articles have been selected to supplement the diverse views presented in this chapter.

John Beisner, "How Much Does Welfare Cost the Average Taxpayer," *Des Moines Register,* May 26, 2016. https://www.desmoinesregister.com/story/opinion/readers/2016/05/26/how-much-does-welfare-cost-average-taxpayer/84917512/.

Marina N. Bolotnikova, "Welfare's Payback," *Harvard Magazine,* November 2020. https://www.harvardmagazine.com/2020/10/right-now-welfare-payback.

Paul Caine, "How Is the US Faring 60 Years After President Lyndon Johnson Declared 'War on Poverty?'," WTTW, January 3, 2024. https://news.wttw.com/2024/01/03/how-us-faring-60-years-after-president-lyndon-johnson-declared-war-poverty.

Ken Coleman, "On This Day in 1964: LBJ Calls for War on Poverty in America," Michigan Advance, January 8, 2024. https://michiganadvance.com/briefs/on-this-day-in-1964-lbj-calls-for-war-on-poverty-in-america/.

Roger E. A. Farmer, "Paying for the Welfare State Without Raising Taxes," Project Syndicate, June 13, 2019. https://www.project-syndicate.org/commentary/national-treasuries-social-care-funds-by-roger-farmer-2019-06.

Andrew Glass, "Clinton Signs Welfare to Work Bill, Aug. 22, 1996," *Politico*, August 22, 2018. https://www.politico.com/story/2018/08/22/clinton-signs-welfare-to-work-bill-aug-22-1996-790321.

Gabriela Goodman and Tara Watson, "How Generous are Each State's Safety Net Programs?" Brookings, November 28, 2023. https://www.brookings.edu/articles/how-generous-are-each-states-safety-net-programs/.

Melissa Kearney, "Welfare and the Federal Budget," Econofact, July 25, 2017. https://econofact.org/welfare-and-the-federal-budget.

Chris McGreal, "Clinton-Era Welfare Reforms Haunt America's Poorest Families Critics Say," the *Guardian*, March 7, 2016.

https://www.theguardian.com/us-news/2016/mar/07/clinton-era-welfare-reforms-american-poor-bernie-sanders.

Vann R. Newkirk, "The Real Lessons from Bill Clinton's Welfare Reform," the *Atlantic,* February 5, 2018. https://www.theatlantic.com/politics/archive/2018/02/welfare-reform-tanf-medicaid-food-stamps/552299/.

CHAPTER 2

Should the Government Be Responsible for Welfare and Social Security Programs?

Chapter Preface

There is no question that a country cannot have a functioning society without a system of social welfare. There will always be the need for a social safety net to provide aid to those who require assistance. The question is whether a country's government should be responsible for providing aid and support and, if so, what kinds of aid and support they should provide. If not the government, then who or what should be responsible for this?

Most individuals work to support themselves and their families after becoming an adult. But what happens to those unable to work, especially through no fault of their own? What if someone becomes ill, or is disabled? What if a natural disaster strikes? And what if a person has no family to support them in tough times? These are all valid questions for a democratic society.

The viewpoints in this chapter debate whether the government should oversee programs aimed at helping disadvantaged or poor individuals and families. One viewpoint argues that a large portion of people in the United States have benefitted from social welfare programs in their own lives, while another disputes the myth of the "welfare queens" who purposely aim to defraud and cheat society to get money and benefits when they don't need them. Another viewpoint explores the possibility that government agencies and individuals are acting on their own behalf and thereby corruptly taking funds that are targeted for the disadvantaged, and another argues that, conversely, citizens are more willing to help one another out than might be expected.

> "The belief that the government has a responsibility to ensure health coverage has increased across many groups over the past year, but the rise has been particularly striking among lower- and middle-income Republicans."

The Government Should Ensure Americans Have Health Coverage

Kristen Bialik

In the following viewpoint Kristen Bialik asserts that a majority of Americans favor a federal government that ensures health care coverage for all citizens, a claim she makes based on the results of a 2017 Pew Research Center survey. Bialik outlines how this manifests across political beliefs and shows the disparate thinking of Democrats and Republicans. Bialik also contends that a large percentage of the population say that the social programs of Medicare and Medicaid should continue. Despite political divisions, the majority of Americans support some government involvement in health care coverage. Kristen Bialik is a former research assistant at Pew Research Center.

"More Americans say government should ensure health care coverage," by Kristen Bialik, Pew Research Center, January 13, 2017.

Welfare and Social Security Programs

As you read, consider the following questions:

1. According to this viewpoint, do Americans as a whole expect the government to ensure health care coverage?
2. Which groups of people most favor a "health coverage for all" approach, according to Bialik?
3. Does income affect opinions about health coverage, according to the data cited in this viewpoint?

As the debate continues over repeal of the Affordable Care Act and what might replace it, a growing share of Americans believe that the federal government has a responsibility to make sure all Americans have health care coverage, according to a new Pew Research Center survey.

What Is Medicaid?

Medicaid is a joint federal-state program that provided health care coverage to an estimated 70.2 million people in fiscal year (FY) 2019. As a major payer in the U.S. health care system, it accounted for about 16.2 percent of national health care spending in calendar year 2019.

Medicaid's role among payers is unique. It provides coverage for health and other related services for the nation's most economically disadvantaged populations, including low-income children and their families, low-income seniors, and low-income people with disabilities. These populations are distinguished by the breadth and intensity of their health needs; the impact of poverty, unemployment, and other socioeconomic factors on their ability to obtain health care services; and the degree to which they require assistance in paying for care. Medicaid provides benefits not typically covered (or covered to a lesser extent) by other insurers, including long-term services and supports.

Currently, 60% of Americans say the government should be responsible for ensuring health care coverage for all Americans, compared with 38% who say this should not be the government's responsibility. The share saying it is the government's responsibility has increased from 51% last year and now stands at its highest point in nearly a decade.

Just as there are wide differences between Republicans and Democrats about the 2010 health care law, the survey also finds partisan differences in views on whether it's the government's responsibility to make sure all Americans have health care coverage. More than eight-in-ten Democrats and Democratic-leaning independents (85%) say the federal government should be responsible for health care coverage, compared with just 32% of Republicans and Republican leaners.

> It also pays for Medicare premiums and cost sharing for more than 12 million people who are enrolled in both programs. It is also a major source of financing for care delivered by certain providers, particularly safety net institutions that serve both low-income and uninsured individuals.
>
> The Medicaid program was enacted as part of the Social Security Amendments of 1965 (P.L. 89-97), the same legislation that created Medicare. Like Medicare, Medicaid is an entitlement program. Eligible individuals have rights to payment for medically necessary health care services defined in statute; the federal government is obligated to fund a share of the outlays for those services.
>
> Variability in Medicaid is the rule rather than the exception. States establish their own eligibility standards, benefit packages, provider payment policies, and administrative structures under broad federal guidelines, effectively creating 56 different Medicaid programs—one for each state, territory, and the District of Columbia. States also differ in Medicaid financing.
>
> "Medicaid 101," the Medicaid and CHIP Payment and Access Commission.

Welfare and Social Security Programs

The survey also finds continued differences on this question by race and ethnicity as well as income. A large majority of Blacks and Hispanics (85% and 84%, respectively) say the government should be responsible for coverage, while non-Hispanic whites are split on the issue (49% agree, 49% disagree). And while about three-quarters of those with family incomes of less than $30,000 per year (74%) say the government should ensure coverage, only about half (53%) of those with incomes of $75,000 or higher say the same.

The belief that the government has a responsibility to ensure health coverage has increased across many groups over the past year, but the rise has been particularly striking among lower- and middle-income Republicans.

Currently, 52% of Republicans with family incomes below $30,000 say the federal government has a responsibility to ensure health coverage for all, up from just 31% last year. There also has been a 20-percentage-point increase among Republicans with incomes of $30,000-$74,999 (34% now, 14% last year). But there has been no significant change among those with incomes of $75,000 or more (18% now, 16% then).

Those who think government should ensure health coverage for all are divided on a follow-up question about whether health insurance should be provided through a mix of private insurance companies and the government (29% of the overall public), or if the government alone should provide insurance (28% of the public).

Overall, 43% of Democrats and Democratic leaners support a so-called single payer approach, but this approach is more popular among liberal Democrats (51%) than among conservative and moderate Democrats (38%).

Most of those on the other side of the issue—people who say the government does *not* have a responsibility to ensure health coverage—say on a subsequent question that the government should continue Medicare and Medicaid (32% of the overall public), while just 5% of the public says the government should have no role in health care.

Among Republicans and Republican leaners, most of whom (67%) say the government does not have a responsibility for ensuring health coverage, there is very little support for the government not being involved in health care at all. Just 10% of Republicans favor no government involvement, while 56% say it should continue Medicare and Medicaid.

While Republicans in Congress have already taken the first steps toward repealing the ACA, Americans remain largely divided on what Congress should do with the health care law. Overall, in a Pew Research Center survey in December, 39% said it should be repealed, while an equal share (39%) said the law should be expanded. Just 15% of Americans said the law should be left as is. Although the public is divided on the future of the law, there is bipartisan support for a number of ACA provisions. Regardless of their personal views of the law, a small majority (53%) expects its major provisions will likely be eliminated.

A December Kaiser Family Foundation survey shows repealing the law is not the public's top health care priority for President-elect Donald Trump and the next Congress. Lowering the amount individuals pay for health care tops the list, with 67% of Americans saying it should be a top priority for the next administration. This is followed by lowering the cost of prescription drugs (61%) and dealing with the prescription-painkiller addiction epidemic (45%). Only 37% of the public says repealing the law should be the administration's top priority, though views differ widely by party.

VIEWPOINT 2

> "The provision of government assistance over an extended period of time could yield high social and economic returns, not least by allowing low-income families to make longer-term investments for the future."

Is the Myth of Welfare Dependency Valid?
Rema Hanna

In the following viewpoint Rema Hanna seeks to dispel myths about the social welfare system. Hanna looks at prevailing attitudes about social welfare and government assistance programs. Many people who are opposed to government welfare programs argue that people who do not actually need help take advantage of them. Hanna and her research team use Indonesia as a case study to demonstrate the role of a positive government intervention. Hanna further outlines the positive results that can occur when a government intervenes correctly. Rema Hanna is the faculty director for the South-East Asia Studies program at the Harvard Kennedy School.

As you read, consider the following questions:

1. Which U.S. president promised to bring an end to typical welfare programs, according to Hanna?

"Dispelling the Myth of Welfare Dependency," by Rema Hanna, Harvard Kennedy School, August 9, 2019. Reprinted by permission.

2. Which segment of the population believes that government assistance leads to dependence, according to this viewpoint?
3. Which country's model of government assistance did the author use for her arguments in the viewpoint?

Social safety nets worldwide routinely come under attack by critics wielding an argument that is as misleading as it is familiar. Measures such as subsidized health insurance, food and nutrition programs, and targeted cash payments to the poor, it is said, incentivize idleness, encourage freeloading, and create a culture of dependency. In response, policymakers cut funding, allow inflation to erode benefits, and make social programs harder for people to access.

In the United States a generation ago, President Bill Clinton's promise to "end welfare as we know it" assumed that income support to the needy generates indigence. Accordingly, his administration drastically reduced transfers and benefit durations, and introduced stiffer eligibility requirements. At the same time, social programs began to include mechanisms to compel labor-market participation, by cutting benefits for able-bodied adults who proved unable or unwilling to find work. The very name of one key new program, *Temporary* Assistance for Needy Families (TANF), emphasized the expectation that support would not be indefinite.

Today, the fixation on dependency and its consequences is no less acute. Following a new directive by the Trump administration, Kentucky, Arkansas, and 14 other U.S. states have announced or introduced work requirements as a condition of eligibility for Medicaid (public health insurance for the poor). According to the administration's statement on the future of the safety net in the United States, the goal is to "lift our citizens from welfare to work, from dependence to independence."

But the idea that government assistance drives dependency is not unique to any country, even if all countries face unique challenges in providing safety nets for the poor. Moreover, beliefs about dependency are not just common among the rich; one often hears similar complaints from the very people whom social programs are meant to help. It is thus little wonder that such beliefs would translate into policy.

That is why it is important to understand how much citizens' attitudes about dependency affect the safety net in their respective countries. Using the World Values Survey, my colleagues and I have assessed how much people attribute poverty to laziness, as opposed to social and economic unfairness, and how it relates to beliefs on redistribution. We find that the more people attribute poverty to a lack of willpower, the less generous the transfer system in their country will be.

Safety Net or Trampoline?

So, beliefs about dependency can have real and tangible implications for the poor and the protections they need. But what if those beliefs are wrong? For example, far from creating dependency, it is possible that welfare programs actually give people the necessary tools to achieve financial independence, provided that the assistance is dependable rather than sporadic and temporary. In that case, the provision of government assistance over an extended period of time could yield high social and economic returns, not least by allowing low-income families to make longer-term investments for the future.

To determine if social programs lead to dependency or independence, my coauthors and I studied the effects of Indonesia's cash-transfer scheme, Program Keluarga Harapan ("Hopeful Family Program"). With the help of the World Bank, the government of Indonesia launched PKH as a large-scale policy experiment in 2008. The program was implemented in 180 randomly selected sub-districts, which were compared to a control group of 180 sub-districts that did not have the program. All told, 14,000 households were surveyed to assess the program's outcomes.

PKH provides quarterly cash transfers to the country's poorest households, roughly meaning those within the bottom 7% of the income distribution. Payments constitute 7–14% of a recipient's income, so they are not meant to cover all of a household's needs. Moreover, the program was directed at families, which were encouraged to use the benefits to invest in their children. Only households with children or a pregnant woman could enroll, and a portion of the stipend was made conditional on fulfilling various health- and education-related obligations, such as basic immunization and the completion of at least nine years of school. As in many countries, these conditions are hard to enforce in practice, so many households received full payments despite non-compliance.

One important feature of PKH is that it did not merely provide a few weeks or months of assistance between jobs or in the case of a financial shock. Rather, it focused on the very poor, and was administered for at least six years, with the understanding that climbing out of poverty takes time and requires consistent support and stability.

Putting Transfers to the Test

In 2011, a study of PKH's initial effects showed that it had a positive impact on short-term indicators of health and educational outcomes after about two years. For example, the program was found to have increased recipients' visits to post-natal care facilities, as well as their enrollment of children in elementary and middle school.

Given this initial success, the Indonesian government expanded the program widely over the next few years. By 2013, it was providing assistance to about 2.3 million households in 3,400 sub-districts across the country. Now, however, the government was targeting specific districts, rather than following the previous random-selection process. As a result, many of the sub-districts in the initial control group were left out, and have not received the program yet.

This offered us a rare opportunity to understand what happens when poor households receive *continued assistance* beyond the scope of their immediate needs, and into what researchers call the "medium run" (in this case, six years). Upon re-surveying the 14,000 households in the original treatment and control groups, we found several interesting outcomes.

The first concerns stunting, or impaired growth, which is one of the most serious child health problems in Indonesia. Because children grow slower when they are malnourished, a child's height relative to their age can serve as a proxy measure of nutrition. Research has shown a correlation between stunting, lower IQs, and poorer socioeconomic outcomes later in life.

At the two-year mark, PKH had no impact on child stunting. And yet, because height is a measure of health that expresses itself cumulatively over time, it was possible that stunting would start to be reversed only after continued assistance from the program. That was precisely what happened. At the six-year mark, children whose families had regularly received extra assistance from PKH were 23–27% less likely than those in the control group to experience stunting.

Back to School

We found similar effects with respect to education. At the two-year mark, PKH had increased school enrollment for children aged 7–15, but not for those aged 15–17. At the time, we reasoned that older children who had dropped out prior to the program would have a harder time returning to school than would their younger counterparts, even if their family resources had recently improved.

But we suspected that if families could benefit from sustained access to the program, their kids would not drop out at an earlier age, with enrollment among those in the 15–17 age bracket thus improving over time. Again, this turned out to be the case. At the six-year mark, children whose families started receiving PKH benefits when they were around 9-11 years old (meaning they were now 15–17 years old) were about 16% more likely to be enrolled in school.

The importance of these improvements in health and education can hardly be overstated. Leaving aside the obvious moral arguments for guaranteeing children access to nutrition and schooling, these investments in low-income households will likely translate into far-reaching economic benefits, including increased labor-market participation and productivity. And that, in turn, could lead to reduced participation in social programs themselves.

In short, Indonesia's cash-transfer program yielded significant improvements in some of the most stubborn and problematic areas of public health and education. More to the point, these gains were made possible by a cumulative investment in children over the course of six years. Most likely, these results would not have been achieved under a program providing temporary or sporadic benefits.

Welfare As We Know It

But the question remains: do such programs create a "culture of dependency"? In the case of PKH, children who grow up healthier and more educated will arguably be better positioned to earn higher incomes and work longer into the future. Of course, to confirm this empirically, we would need to follow the original sample population into adulthood as they enter the workforce and develop careers.

In the meantime, critics will doubtless argue that the program creates dependency for able-bodied adults today. And they might even contend that the culture of dependency will be reproduced inter-generationally, as parents' attitudes about not working and "being on the dole" are passed down to their children.

Yet here it is worth taking a step back and exploring where the idea of welfare dependency comes from in the first place. We know that beliefs about dependency, laziness, and voluntary unemployment among the poor are pervasive. But why is that?

The primary culprit seems to be classical economic theory, which predicts that when governments provide benefits, individuals may decide that they can afford to work less (economists refer to this as the "income effect"). Similarly, if recipients worry about losing eligibility for benefits if they earn more, they may abstain from work. It is this moral hazard that supposedly leads people to remain poor and rely on welfare indefinitely.

But the evidence does not always support this theory. In another study, my colleagues and I re-analyzed data from seven different experimental trials of government cash-transfer programs throughout the developing world, from the Philippines to Morocco to Mexico. We found that in most cases, men who received benefits tended to be working already, and that there was no evidence that systematic income support reduced work. In an even more recent study, Sarah Jane Baird, David J. McKenzie, and Berk Özler of the World Bank undertook a systematic review of the economics literature on this topic and came to a similar conclusion.

As for PKH, we did not find that program recipients stopped working, even after six years of receiving cash transfers.

From "Dependency" to Dependable

To be sure, some social programs might well reduce work. Obviously, policymakers should consider the downstream effects of public benefits on labor markets and other areas of the economy. At the same time, the way we think and talk about "dependency" needs to change. The claim that transfers necessarily reduce work may hold true in Economics 101; in the real world, much depends on context and how policies are designed and implemented in practice.

It's time to bring our beliefs about dependency into line with the data. There is an extensive and growing body of evidence from around the world showing that even very simple cash-transfer programs need not have adverse effects on work.

More broadly, we should focus less on policing "freeloaders," and more on giving poor families the type of dependable financial assistance that will allow them to make substantial long-run investments in the health and education of their children. As

Should the Government Be Responsible for Welfare and Social Security Programs?

we have seen, the returns on such investments are real, and will accumulate over time.

If we are willing to cast aside the prevailing beliefs about poor people's "dependency" and "laziness," we can start to make the social safety net a springboard of upward social mobility.

VIEWPOINT 3

> "The survey also finds that most Democrats (60%) and Republicans (52%) say they have benefited from a major entitlement program at some point in their lives. So have nearly equal shares of self-identifying conservatives (57%), liberals (53%) and moderates (53%)."

Many Americans Have Received Government Benefits

Rich Morin, Paul Taylor, and Eileen Patten

In the following viewpoint, Rich Morin, Paul Taylor, and Eileen Patten outline the prevalence of social welfare assistance in the United States. The authors provide ample statistics to show which groups in the United States receive the most benefits, and which groups favor government assistance. Despite the fact that certain groups tend to receive more benefits, the data suggests that all types of Americans have made use of government benefits. Rich Morin is a former senior editor, Paul Taylor is former vice president, and Eileen Patten is a former research analyst, all at Pew Research Center.

"A Bipartisan Nation of Beneficiaries," by Rich Morin, Paul Taylor and Eileen Patten, Pew Research Center, December 18, 2012.

Should the Government Be Responsible for Welfare and Social Security Programs?

As you read, consider the following questions:

1. What percent of Americans have received government benefits at some point in their lives, according to this viewpoint?
2. According to the authors, which three populations in the United States receive social welfare assistance at higher rates than other groups?
3. Which social assistance programs are the most widely used, according to this viewpoint?

As President Barack Obama negotiates with Republicans in Congress over federal entitlement spending, a new national survey by the Pew Research Center finds that a majority of Americans (55%) have received government benefits from at least one of the six best-known federal entitlement programs.

The survey also finds that most Democrats (60%) and Republicans (52%) say they have benefited from a major entitlement program at some point in their lives. So have nearly equal shares of self-identifying conservatives (57%), liberals (53%) and moderates (53%).

The issue of entitlements moved to center stage during the 2012 presidential campaign. The survey finds that among those who voted for President Obama last month, 59% say they've benefited from a major entitlement program. It also finds that 53% of those who supported Mitt Romney have benefited from a major entitlement program.

The survey, which was conducted by telephone from Nov. 28 to Dec. 5, 2012, among a nationally representative sample of 2,511 adults, asked respondents if they or a member of their household had ever received Social Security, Medicare, Medicaid, food stamps, welfare or unemployment benefits. Margin of sampling error for the overall results is plus or minus 2.2 percentage points.

Some 55% said they personally had received benefits from at least one of those programs, including a third (32%) who said they had received help from two or more. An additional 16% said they themselves had not received any benefits but said that a member of their household had—meaning that 71% of adults are part of a household that has benefited from at least one of these programs.[1]

The survey finds that the ranks of beneficiaries are as diverse as the nation as a whole but that there are some notable group differences. For example, women are more likely than men to have received an entitlement benefit (61% vs. 49%). Blacks (64%) are more likely than whites (56%) or Hispanics (50%) to have gotten federal help from these programs, and rural residents (62%) are more likely than urban (54%) or suburban (53%) dwellers to have gotten help.

The use of entitlement begins at an early age for many Americans, the survey finds. A third (33%) of all adults ages 18 to 29 say they have received at least one major entitlement payment or service in their lives.[2]

The share that has used entitlements continues to rise steadily with age, growing to 45% among those ages 30 to 49 and to 59% for those ages 50 to 64. It becomes virtually universal (97%) among those ages 65 and older—the age at which most adults qualify for Social Security and Medicare benefits.

According to the survey, 32% of all adults have received two or more benefits, including 15% who have received three or more. Blacks are more likely than whites or Hispanics to have received three or more benefits (27% vs. 14% for whites and 11% for Hispanics).

The survey also finds that nearly six-in-ten Americans (57%) say it is the government's responsibility to care for those who cannot take care of themselves, a view that is only slightly more prevalent among those who have ever received an entitlement benefit (60%) than among those who have not (55%).

Taken together, the six programs tested in this survey generate the vast majority of federal spending on what is often called the social safety net. But each one has a different purpose and target population.

Unemployment benefits, food stamps, welfare and Medicaid target lower-income Americans or those facing a short-term economic hardship such as the loss of a job. In contrast, Social Security and Medicare primarily—though not exclusively—serve older adults of all income levels.

Overall, four-in-ten adults (42%) say they have been helped by a program targeted to assist those facing financial hardship. A smaller share (30%) say they have received a Social Security or Medicare benefit. About one-in-six Americans (17%) say they have received benefits from both types of programs at some point in their lives.

Blacks are more likely than whites to have benefited from one of the four economic hardship programs, but the survey suggests there are no statistically significant differences by race in participation over time in Social Security and Medicare.

Predictably, adults 65 and older are far more likely than other age group to have received Social Security and Medicare.

Adults with annual family incomes of less than $30,000 are about three times as likely as those earning $100,000 or more to have received help from Social Security or Medicare. These programs do not have income eligibility requirements: the fact that a larger share of recipients are at the lower end of the income scale reflects the fact that older adults tend to have lower incomes than the general public.

The survey also finds that these low-earning adults are nearly twice as likely as the highest earners to have received some sort of benefit from a poverty program, including unemployment insurance (59% vs. 31%).

The Reach of Entitlement Programs

More than half (55%) of Americans have personally received benefits from at least one of the six major entitlement programs tested in the survey.

The survey finds that 16% of those who have not personally received benefits also say a member of their household has gotten help. Taken together, these results indicate that about seven-in-ten households contain at least one member who has benefited at some point in his or her life from an entitlement program.

If veteran benefits and federal college loans and grants are added to the mix, the proportion of Americans who personally have ever received entitlement benefits rises to 70% and the share of households with at least one recipient grows to 86%.

Most Utilized Programs

In terms of utilization, unemployment benefits and Social Security top the list of the six entitlement programs that are the focus of this analysis.

About one-in-four adults (27%) say they have received unemployment assistance at some point in their lives.[3] About as many (26%) have received Social Security, while 22% have used Medicare. Smaller shares have ever received food stamps (18%), Medicaid (11%) or welfare benefits (8%).

The Demographics of Entitlements

The beneficiaries of entitlements span the social, political and economic spectrum. But some group differences do emerge. Women are more likely than men to have received an entitlement benefit (61% vs. 49%). Blacks (64%) are somewhat more likely than whites (56%) or Hispanics (50%) to have gotten federal help of this kind.

Rural residents also have disproportionately benefited from these entitlements (62%), compared with urban (54%) or suburban (53%) dwellers.

While the two parties are sharply divided over entitlement spending, the differences in the proportions of Republicans and Democrats who have received entitlements is fairly modest: 60% of Democrats, 52% of Republicans and 53% of independents have benefited from one of these six major classes of federal entitlement programs.

And when the lens shifts to political ideology, the survey finds virtually no difference in the share of conservatives (57%), liberals (53%) or political moderates (53%) who have been assisted by at least one entitlement program.

Taken together, the last two findings help explain another result. In the recent presidential election, about six-in-ten (59%) of those who say they voted for President Obama had received entitlement benefits—and so had 53% of those who supported Republican challenger Mitt Romney.

Program Goals and Demographics

Larger group differences emerge when the results are broken down by age and income levels—differences that are often directly related to the goals of specific benefits programs.

For example, adults 65 and older are nearly three times as likely to have received an entitlement benefit during their lives as those adults under the age of 30 (97% vs. 33%). That's not surprising, since nearly nine-in-ten older adults (88%) have received Social Security and 78% have gotten Medicare benefits. Both programs were specifically created for seniors with age requirements that limit participation by younger adults.

Similarly, Americans with family incomes of less than $30,000 a year are significantly more likely as those with family incomes of $100,000 or more to have gotten entitlement help from the government (70% vs. 39%). Again, this difference is not surprising, as assisting the poor is the primary objective of such financial means-tested programs as food stamps, welfare assistance and Medicaid.

Type of Entitlement and Demographics

The survey finds that, overall, more Americans have received entitlements from programs primarily designed for the poor or unemployed (42%) than from those that mainly target older adults (30%), while 17% have received benefits from both program types. Not surprisingly, the biggest difference in the demographic profiles of the two groups is the age of recipients.

Adults 65 and older are nearly eight times as likely as adults younger than 30 to receive assistance targeting older Americans (94% vs. 12%).[4] But among those who received poverty entitlements, the generation gap narrows to 13 percentage points (43% vs. 30%). While adults 65 and older are still more likely than young people to have benefited from these programs, those 30 to 49 are about as likely as those 65 and older to have received this type of entitlement. Fully half of all 50- to 64-year-olds, the largest share of any age group, have received a poverty entitlement.

On other demographic comparisons, the differences are less dramatic and the patterns less consistent. In fact, despite the very different goals of these two classes of entitlement programs, the demographic patterns in one class of entitlement programs often are roughly mirrored in the other. For example, women are more likely than men to say they have received help from programs that benefited the poor (46% vs. 38%) as well as from those that target older adults (33% vs. 26%).

Less affluent Americans adults also are significantly more likely than those in higher income brackets to have received entitlements, regardless of program class. About six-in-ten (59%) of those with family incomes of $30,000 or less say they have gotten this kind of help, compared with 31% of those earning $100,000 or more. If anything, the income gap is even larger among those who have received Social Security or Medicare (41% vs. 14%).

Other demographic groups show a mixed pattern by class of assistance. Rural residents are more likely than those living in the suburbs to have received entitlements, regardless of the type of assistance. However, there is no significant difference between rural and urban residents among those who have gotten poverty entitlements (47% vs. 43%), though there is a difference between those who received Social Security or Medicare (38% of rural vs. 28% of urban).

As for political characteristics, Democrats are more likely than Republicans or independents to have received poverty or unemployment assistance (47% vs. 34% and 41%, respectively).

But Republicans and Democrats are about equally likely to have gotten Social Security or Medicare benefits (32% vs. 33%). Independents are significantly less likely (25%) than partisans from either party to say they benefited from entitlement programs for the elderly. Despite conservatives' opposition to many poverty programs, there is virtually no difference in the lifetime participation rate of conservatives (40%), liberals (42%) and moderates (42%) in these programs. Also, conservatives are more likely to have gotten Social Security and Medicare (34% vs. 27% for liberals and 25% for moderates), a difference driven by the fact that self-identifying conservatives are the oldest of the three groups.

Multiple Benefits

About a third of all Americans (32%) have benefited from two or more entitlement programs over the course of their lives: 17% have been helped by two programs and 15% have received assistance from three or more.

In general, the characteristics of those who have received entitlements from multiple sources echo the overall demographic pattern described earlier: more likely to be Black, female, have a lower income, identify with the Democratic Party or live in a rural area.

A plurality of Blacks (44%), but 33% of whites and 23% of Latinos, received entitlements from two or more of the six programs tested in the survey.[5] About a quarter of all Blacks

(27%) received entitlements from three or more programs; in contrast, 14% of whites and 11% of Hispanics received help from as many government sources. (As a group, Hispanics experience similar levels of economic hardship as Blacks. Their lower utilization of entitlement benefits stems in part from their relative youth and in part from the fact that some are in the country illegally and thus unable to receive benefits.)

Women are significantly more likely than men to have ever received two or more entitlements. According to the survey, about four-in-ten (38%) of all women and 26% of men got help from two or more of the six major entitlement programs.

Lower-income adults are more than three times as likely to receive entitlements from multiple programs as the more affluent (50% for those with family incomes under $30,000 vs. 14% among those making $100,000 a year or more).

Democrats (37%) are more likely than Republicans (30%) or independents (28%) to have received entitlements from two or more government programs.

What Is Government's Role in Caring For the Most Needy?

Nearly six-in-ten Americans (57%) say government has a responsibility to take care of those who cannot take care of themselves. Do these views vary depending on whether the respondent has personally benefited from a government entitlement program?

These data suggest the answer is a qualified yes. Overall, those who have received benefits from at least one of the six major programs are somewhat more likely than those who haven't to say government is responsible for caring for those who cannot help themselves (60% vs. 55%).

When the analysis focuses just on just the respondents who have received benefits from at least one of the four programs that target the needy, the gap between entitlement recipients and other adults increases to eight percentage points (62% vs. 54%).

Some larger differences in attitudes toward government's role emerge when the results are broken down by specific program, though in every case majorities of both recipients and non-recipients affirmed that government has the obligation to help those most in need.

For example, nearly three-quarters of those who ever received welfare benefits (73%) say government has a duty to care for those who cannot care for themselves. In contrast, less than six-in-ten (56%) of those who have never been on welfare agree.

Similar double-digit gaps surface between non-recipients and those who ever received food stamps (14 percentage points) and Medicaid (13 points).

But when those who ever received unemployment benefits are compared with those who have not, the gap virtually disappears: About six-in-ten adults (57%) who have received unemployment benefits say government should help the helpless, while 58% who never collected jobless benefits agree.

No significant differences in attitudes toward government's responsibility to the neediest emerged between adults who have ever received Social Security and those who have not (60% vs. 57%). Similarly about six-in-ten (61%) of those who benefited from Medicare believe it is government's duty to help those who cannot help themselves, while 56% of those who have not received these benefits agree.

The survey finds a big difference by partisanship on this question. Nearly three-quarters (74%) of Democrats say the government has such a responsibility compared with 57% of independents and 38% of Republicans.

Notes

1. Respondents were asked "whether you or anyone in your household has ever received any of the following government services and benefits": Social Security, Medicare, Medicaid, welfare, unemployment benefits, food stamps, college grants and loans, and veteran benefits. Those who answered yes they alone had received the benefit and those who said they and someone else had received it were coded as having received the benefit. Those who answered no, refused to answer or said they did not know were coded as not having received the benefit.

Welfare and Social Security Programs

2. Respondents could have received benefits as an adult or when they were a child. The question did not ask respondents how old they were when they received an entitlement.
3. The 27% includes 23% who personally received unemployment benefits but live in a household where no other household member did and 4% who got unemployment and a household member did as well.
4. Some disabled workers, survivors of workers and other family members of disabled or retired workers are eligible for Social Security, as are adults beginning at age 62.
5. The total of those who received two and three or more benefits may differ by 1 percentage point from the chart due to rounding.]

VIEWPOINT 4

> "To people who were opposed to welfare, Taylor's colorful transgressions were evidence of just how little oversight there was in the program and how easily it could be abused."

Are There People Who Take Advantage of Public Assistance?

Gene Demby

In the following viewpoint Gene Demby puts a face on what many conservatives call the "welfare queen," a person (typically a woman) who willingly defrauds governmental agencies while getting monetary assistance. Demby paints the true-life story of such a woman. Demby outlines the partial life story of a woman who was remarkably adept at posing as different people to get what she wanted and the ways in which her story helped shape many of the misconceptions about the welfare system that persist today. Gene Demby is a co-host and correspondent for NPR's Code Switch podcast.

©2013 National Public Radio, Inc. NPR news report "The Truth Behind the Lies of The Original 'Welfare Queen'" by Gene Demby was originally published on npr.org on December 20, 2013, and is used with the permission of NPR. Any unauthorized duplication is strictly prohibited.

Welfare and Social Security Programs

As you read, consider the following questions:

1. According to Demby, how does Linda Taylor not align with the stereotype of the "welfare queen"?
2. What were two different disguises Linda Taylor used as reported in the viewpoint?
3. From the examples in the viewpoint, is Taylor a criminal?

If you haven't read Josh Levin's amazing story at *Slate*—the woman upon whom the term "welfare queen" was originally bestowed—you're missing out on a fascinating and disturbing profile of an unlikely political figure. Linda Taylor was never mentioned by name, but she was the subject of many of Ronald Reagan's 1976 presidential campaign speech anecdotes about a Chicago woman who'd defrauded the government of hundreds of thousands of dollars. And while Reagan's critics on the left argued that the woman was a fabrication, Levin reminds us at length that she wasn't.

If Taylor was a character in a movie, people would dismiss her as an implausibility. She really did bilk various government programs of hundreds of thousands of dollars. She also burned through husbands, sometimes more than one at a time. She was a master of disguise, armed with dozens of wigs. She flipped through assumed and fake identities and employed 33 known aliases; Levin said that he refers to her as "Linda Taylor" because that was the name she was known by at the time of her high-profile trial for fraud. She enchanted and charmed some of her marks, while others were deathly afraid of her.

But Levin's story isn't merely fascinating. It also deepens our understanding of the narratives and reality around welfare.

The Racial Ideas That Don't Neatly Line Up

In the popular imagination, the stereotype of the "welfare queen" is thoroughly racist—she's an indolent Black woman, living off the largesse of taxpayers. The term is seen by many as a dogwhistle, a way to play on racial anxieties without summoning them directly.

Taylor's own racial reality is much harder to pin down, however. Born Martha Miller, she was listed as white in the 1930 Census, just like everyone else in her family. But she had darker skin and darker hair. People who knew her family told Levin that she had Native American ancestry. One of her husbands, who was Black, said she could look like an Asian woman at times. Another earlier husband and ostensible father to some of her children was white, and during that marriage she gave birth to kids who alternately appeared Black, unmistakably white, or racially ambiguous. At times she posed as a Jewish woman. In one photo, she has long, blonde hair.

"She was white according to official records and in the view of certain family members who couldn't imagine it any other way," Levin writes. "She was Black (or colored, or a Negro) when it suited her needs, or when someone saw a woman they didn't think, or didn't want to think, could possibly be Caucasian."

Living Off the System

To people who were opposed to welfare, Taylor's colorful transgressions were evidence of just how little oversight there was in the program and how easily it could be abused. (In reality, Taylor stole her money from a host of government services, and defrauded private individuals, too.)

So how much fraud is there really in the welfare system? As Eric Schnurer writes at *The Atlantic*, it's actually not so clear.

> It's not easy to get agreement on actual fraud levels in government programs. Unsurprisingly, liberals say they're low, while conservatives insist they're astronomically high. In truth, it varies from program to program. One government report says fraud accounts for less than 2 percent of unemployment insurance payments. It's seemingly impossible to find statistics on "welfare" (i.e., TANF) fraud, but the best guess is that it's about the same. A bevy of inspector general reports found "improper payment"

levels of 20 to 40 percent in state TANF programs—but when you look at the reports, the payments appear all to be due to bureaucratic incompetence (categorized by the inspector general as either "eligibility and payment calculation errors" or "documentation errors"), rather than intentional fraud by beneficiaries.

Levin cites an old government report from a few years after Taylor's fraud trial estimating the amount of overpayment in the Aid to Families with Dependent Children program to be somewhere between $376 million and $3.2 billion. Even back then, when welfare fraud was getting a ton of press attention, the figures were wildly unclear.

"What's clear, though, is that Linda Taylor's larger-than-life example created an indelible, inaccurate impression of public aid recipients," Levin writes. "Linda Taylor showed that it was possible for a dedicated criminal to steal a healthy chunk of welfare money. Her case did not prove that, as a group, public aid recipients were fur-laden thieves bleeding the American economy dry."

Taylor's Other Crimes Were Much, Much Worse

The extent of Taylor's lies and the ostentatious way she committed them made her the perfect face for arguments about profligate welfare cheats. But compared to the constellation of offenses Taylor may have committed or abetted, her fraud looks almost tame.

There were the kidnappings. For years, Taylor would take children from parents who made the mistake of trusting her. She was even suspected in the Fronczak kidnapping, one of the most notorious child abductions of the 1960s. In that case, a woman dressed as a nurse snatched a newborn baby and fled.

> Johnnie says his mother often claimed that she worked in a hospital, and that she'd wear a nurse's hat. Rose Termini, without any prompting, begins the narrative of her son's kidnapping by saying that Taylor "once told me she was a nurse and she got around a lot with kids." According to Termini, Taylor would

often dress in a white uniform—she says she saw the getup with her own eyes.

In 1977, a man named Samuel Harper told police prior to Taylor's sentencing for welfare fraud that he believed she had kidnapped Paul Joseph Fronczak. He explained that he was living with her at the time, that several other white infants were in her home, and that she left the house in a white uniform on the day of the kidnapping.

And there were the deaths. Taylor posed as a voodoo practitioner and spiritual adviser, and after one of Taylor's particularly naive marks during that scheme turned up dead, Taylor was found with the dead woman's credit card. But police investigators didn't go after Taylor on murder charges, because they were worried it would detract from an ongoing welfare fraud case.

"Linda Taylor's story shows that there are real costs associated with this kind of panic, a moral climate in which stealing welfare money takes precedence over kidnapping and homicide," Levin writes."

If you have time for only one long read this weekend, you should really holler at Levin's mesmerizing story of this colorful, maddening figure who somehow became central to one our country's most intractable and racially charged policy debates.

VIEWPOINT 5

> "While Republican leadership says it has cleaned up fraud within the agency, that doesn't mean the welfare program, called Temporary Assistance for Needy Families, is reaching the needy or helping people enter the workforce."

The Government Needs to Fix Corruption in State Social Service Programs

Anna Wolfe

In the following viewpoint Anna Wolfe exposes the corruption occurring in the social welfare programs of the state of Mississippi. Wolfe attempts to uncover the blatant corruption that has occurred and appears to be continuing. This sort of fraud suggests that the issue with government welfare programs is not the recipients defrauding the government out of money, but government officials who are misallocating funds. Greater oversight in how grants are spent on benefit programs would help make these programs more effective and cost-efficient. Anna Wolfe is a Pulitzer Prize winning investigative reporter.

"State leaders still won't fix scandalous welfare program that serves few poor families," by Anna Wolfe, Nonprofit Mississippi News, February 17, 2023. https://mississippitoday.org/2023/02/17/poor-families-welfare-scandal/. Licensed under CC-BY ND 4.0 International.

Should the Government Be Responsible for Welfare and Social Security Programs?

As you read, consider the following questions:

1. How many people live below the poverty line in Mississippi, according to this viewpoint?
2. How is the governmental money being spent in Mississippi as reported by Wolfe?
3. According to the experts cited in this viewpoint, what three things keep Mississippians from escaping poverty?

Now that Mississippi's welfare department isn't hemorrhaging federal grant funds as a result of widespread mismanagement and political corruption, it has over $100 million to spare.

But the agency, Mississippi Department of Human Services, won't say what it's going to do with the money, whether it's going to try to reach more needy families or how it's going to finally start tracking outcomes of the program.

In the three years following arrests in the largest public fraud scandal in state history, the agency led by Gov. Tate Reeves has never released a full accounting of its current welfare expenditures. There isn't even a list of organizations receiving the funding on the agency's website, nor are its subgrant agreements available online.

And lawmakers, in their seventh week of the legislative session, haven't taken one action to address the logjam. Instead, they've killed at least 11 bills aimed at improving the administration of the agency and its funds, as well as at least five amendments offered to do the same on the floors of both chambers.

All the bills filed to address these problems were killed by Republican committee chairs without debate, and all the amendments were introduced by Democrats and voted down by Republicans, primarily along party lines.

"(Mississippi Department of Human Services) has certainly not held up to its mission or its responsibility to those who need it the most," said Rep. Omeria Scott, D-Jones, who offered an amendment to the MDHS appropriations bill on Wednesday to make increases to the agency's budget, which Republicans reduced. "I do hate that through the general bills process that there was no legislation for a board, or no legislation for any of these audits that are in this appropriations bill, that we got any reports or any demands or anything like that. That has not been before us, and I imagine won't be before us, but let me say to you that there are areas over there in Human Services that need some escalation."

While Republican leadership says it has cleaned up fraud within the agency, that doesn't mean the welfare program, called Temporary Assistance for Needy Families, is reaching the needy or helping people enter the workforce. In fact, during the height of the scandal, the state was using more of its TANF funds to help more poor Mississippians than it is today.

In 2022, a monthly average of 246 adults and 2,265 children benefited from the welfare check—no more than $260 for a family of three (a rate that was raised in 2021 for the first time since 1999). Mississippi is consistently among the most impoverished states in the nation with 1-in-5 of its residents living below the poverty line. The assistance is reaching about 4% of the more than half-a-million Mississippians living in poverty.

Meanwhile, the state continues to rack up tens of millions in welfare funds. By October of 2021, more than a year ago, Mississippi's TANF program had amassed $97.9 million in unobligated funds. While the agency hasn't released data showing how they spent the money within the last year, all indications are that the number of unspent TANF funds has only grown, especially since the state didn't issue a single new TANF subgrant in 2022.

Should the Government Be Responsible for Welfare and Social Security Programs?

In October, MDHS Director Bob Anderson hesitated to say how his agency might spend the money, or whether it would use the funds to, for example, increase the number of child care vouchers it is able to provide to low-income families.

"Understand, people have a lot of other plans for that money as well," Anderson said.

MDHS has refused to answer Mississippi Today's questions about which people and what plans.

The sections of the TANF program that have received most public attention are:

- Cash assistance—the money that goes out directly to families who qualify for the welfare check
- Subgrants—the money that goes to organizations to provide TANF-related services, such as after-school programs, parenting classes and workforce training

But these currently account for less than half of the state's annual federal TANF grant.

And according to the state's checkbook, the state spends millions of TANF funds each year on items outside of cash assistance or TANF subgrants—such as IT contracts, a contract with the company who conducts drug testing of welfare applicants, interagency transfers to the state auditor's office or payments to the attorneys crafting the civil case against NFL legend Brett Favre and others. There has not been a public accounting of these purchases, nor have they been discussed in audits, legislative hearings or among lawmakers publicly.

Each year, the state also transfers a large chunk of TANF funds, the amount unknown to the public, to Mississippi Child Protection Services, the embattled state agency responsible for investigating child abuse and neglect and overseeing foster care across the state. The financial maneuver is preventing the state from taking advantage of unprecedented federal matching funds offered under the 2018 Family First Prevention Services Act to help families stay intact.

Welfare and Social Security Programs

Aside from the scandalous stories about politicians and famous athletes funneling TANF money to their pet projects during former Gov. Phil Bryant's administration, the welfare program itself is as forgotten and ignored as it was before the arrests.

Lawmakers passed a bill in 2021 to place law enforcement officers within MDHS's Fraud Investigation Unit and a bill in 2022 to require that employees of the unit report civil or criminal violations to the state auditor's office.

Neither of these changed how the agency runs its TANF grant or introduced any accountability for the agency to spend the money effectively.

In 2021, the first full year after the scandal was revealed, Mississippi spent just $35.6 million of the $86.5 million it receives in federal funds each year, according to federal reports released in December. The reports are typically outdated by about a year.

To put that into perspective: In 2018, Mississippi spent about $113 million in federal TANF funds (including some unspent funds from years before). If $50 million of that went to fraudulent or unallowed purchases, that leaves $63 million that Mississippi spent legally that year, including to organizations similar to those providing services today.

In 2018, at the height of the fraud scandal, the state pumped $7.3 million directly to families, whereas it only gave $3.5 million in cash assistance in 2021. Either way you slice it, Mississippi's welfare department was using more TANF money to help more poor Mississippians during the years of Bryant's appointed former MDHS Director John Davis, who is likely going to prison, than the agency is today under Reeves and Anderson.

Mississippi Department of Human Services previously told the public that it is allocating about $69 million of its TANF funds each year—$4.1 million on cash assistance, $34.5 million on subgrants to organizations and $30 million to plug budget holes at the Mississippi Department of Child Protection Services.

But it has not made documentation of these expenditures available to the public. Also, these figures are not clearly reflected in federal reports. In 2021, for example, the state only reported spending $15 million in TANF funds on "child welfare" – the only spending category that would appear to correspond with the CPS transfers.

The agency would not explain the reason for the discrepancies in the federal reporting, other than to say that it's possible not all of the money that the state obligated was actually used. The department has also repeatedly failed to explain which purchases fall under which categories in the federal reports.

The state is allowed to use grant funds from one year to another for a period of three years. So funds being spent today could technically be coming from the state's 2021 TANF grant. That, and the fact that some subgrants span more than one year, during which the subgrantee can draw the funds at their leisure, have perpetually created a foggy picture of the program.

The only documentation of TANF expenditures that MDHS appears to have made public, at the request of Mississippi Today, is a list of subgrantees to whom the state awards a fraction of the funds. This information does not appear on the agency's website, nor in its annual report.

In mid-2020, the department provided to Mississippi Today a spreadsheet of TANF purchases that included, in addition to payments to subgrantees, expenditures for things like tech support or hotels for employee training. In October, Mississippi Today extracted and analyzed all purchases labeled under the TANF program from the state's accounting database from 2015 to 2022, all of which Mississippi Today made publicly available, but the expenditures didn't add up to nearly the amount the state reported spending to the federal government.

Transfers from MDHS to CPS also do not appear on the state's accounting database.

The department began the most recent Request for Proposals—a competitive bid process—for TANF subgrants in June of 2022. But due to staff changes within MDHS's Division of Workforce Development and Partnership Management, a spokesperson said, the agency has not made an award.

"Once we have a finalized plan we will make a public announcement," MDHS Chief Communication Officer Mark Jones offered in response to questions about the agency's plan for the TANF program moving forward.

Even with the grants most recently awarded in 2021, it's unclear what all of the organizations are accomplishing or how the programs align with a vision to reduce poverty. The current grants cover parenting initiatives ($8.1 million), after-school programs ($13.7 million), and workforce development ($14.9 million). The subgrant agreements aren't even available on Mississippi's transparency website.

The largest award was a $6.9 million parenting initiative grant to Mississippi Children's Home Society, or Canopy Solutions, a children's behavioral health services provider, including a residential psychiatric facility. Canopy has been a TANF subgrantee for years and works within the foster care system to prevent family separations. Canopy also recently launched a specialized nonprofit school for students with learning differences in Ridgeland, essentially replacing the recently shuttered New Summit School by hiring its employees and recruiting its students.

New Summit closed after its founder Nancy New was charged within the welfare scandal. New was funneling TANF money to New Summit, a for-profit school, and also running a separate scam to defraud the Mississippi Department of Education, she admitted in her 2022 guilty pleas.

Other current TANF subgrantees include the Mississippi Alliance of Boys and Girls Clubs ($5.3 million), Save the

Children Federation ($2.4 million), YMCA Metro Jackson ($1 million), and Juanita Sims Doty Foundation ($1 million) for afterschool programs; and Institutions of Higher Learning ($2.4 million), Mississippi Department of Employment Security ($1.5 million), South Delta Planning and Development District ($2.1 million), Southern MS Planning and Development District Gulfport ($3.6 million), Three Rivers Planning & Development District ($4.7 million) for workforce training.

Since welfare reform in the late 1990s, state leaders, workforce specialists, industry experts and advocates have met, studied, and discussed ad nauseam the barriers they've identified for families escaping poverty—chief among them child care, transportation and workforce training that aligns with market needs. The concept of TANF when Congress created it was to move people into the workforce, hopefully ending the reliance on government assistance.

Mississippi could be transferring up to 30% of its TANF funding to supplement the Child Care Development Block Grant, which provides child care vouchers to low-income working parents. The program has always served just a small fraction of low-income children needing child care across the state.

While legislation is not required for MDHS to make this transfer – since it has done so in the past, according to federal reports – the current Legislature has killed bills and amendments to compel MDHS to use TANF funds this way. And the agency refuses to answer questions about whether it will or, if not, why it won't. The agency has, however, complained that without a budget supplement, 12,000 kids may be kicked off the voucher.

"From the beginning of the (TANF) program, there have been thoughts like, 'We need to figure out a way to provide daycare. We need to figure out a way to provide transportation and that will help get a large number of people back into the workforce,' which is said to be the aim of all these reforms,"

Welfare and Social Security Programs

Senate Public Health Committee Chair Hob Bryan, D-Amory, said during a floor debate on several TANF-related amendments last week. "And it is extremely frustrating that we have money that could be used for additional vouchers for childcare, so that there would be someone to care for children when their parent is at work and we're not taking advantage of that. And yet we complain about people not working."

VIEWPOINT 6

> "People want to make a difference in people's lives and they feel good—happy even—when they are able to help others"

As a Society, We Should Be Able to Ask One Another for Help

Melissa De Witte

In the following viewpoint Melissa De Witte interviews social psychologist Xuan Zhao about the topic of helping others. De Witte maintains that many people want to help others and often feel good for doing so, but that people have a difficult time asking others for assistance in times of need. De Witte contends that there are ways to rethink our attitudes about asking for help from others and that this reassessing of attitudes would benefit society. The government alone should not be responsible for handling societal issues—we should also help one another handle them. Melissa De Witte was a writer for Stanford News.

As you read, consider the following questions:

1. According to the author, why do people shy away from asking for help?
2. What is the SMART criteria, as explained by De Witte?

"Asking for help is hard, but people want to help more than we realize, Stanford scholar says," by Melissa De Witte, Stanford University, September 8, 2022. Reprinted by permission.

3. According to Zhao, what change in cultural norms would be beneficial?

Asking for help is hard, but others want to help more than we often give them credit for, says Stanford social psychologist Xuan Zhao.

We shy away from asking for help because we don't want to bother other people, assuming that our request will feel like an inconvenience to them. But oftentimes, the opposite is true: People want to make a difference in people's lives and they feel good—happy even—when they are able to help others, said Zhao.

Here, Zhao discusses the research about how asking for help can lead to meaningful experiences and strengthen relationships with others—friends as well as strangers.

Zhao is a research scientist at Stanford SPARQ, a research center in the psychology department that brings researchers and practitioners together to fight bias, reduce disparities, and drive culture change. Zhao's research focuses on helping people create better social interactions in person and online where they feel seen, heard, connected, and appreciated. Her research, recently published in *Psychological Science*, suggests that people regularly underestimate others' willingness to help.

Why is asking for help hard? For someone who finds it difficult to ask for help, what would you like them to know?

There are several common reasons why people struggle to ask for help. Some people may fear that asking for help would make them appear incompetent, weak, or inferior – recent research from Stanford doctoral student Kayla Good finds that children as young as 7 can hold this belief. Some people are concerned about being rejected, which can be embarrassing and painful. Others may be concerned about burdening and inconveniencing others—a topic I recently explored. These concerns may feel more relevant in some contexts than others, but they are all very relatable and very human.

The good news is those concerns are oftentimes exaggerated and mistaken.

What do people misunderstand about asking for help?

When people are in need of help, they are often caught up in their own concerns and worries and do not fully recognize the prosocial motivations of those around them who are ready to help. This can introduce a persistent difference between how help-seekers and potential helpers consider the same helping event. To test this idea, we conducted several experiments where people either directly interacted with each other to seek and offer help, or imagined or recalled such experiences in everyday life. We consistently observed that help-seekers underestimated how willing strangers—and even friends—would be to help them and how positive helpers would feel afterward, and overestimated how inconvenienced helpers would feel.

These patterns are consistent with work by Stanford psychologist Dale Miller showing that when thinking about what motivates other people, we tend to apply a more pessimistic, self-interested view about human nature. After all, Western societies tend to value independence, so asking others to go out of their way to do something for us may seem wrong or selfish and may impose a somewhat negative experience on the helper.

The truth is, most of us are deeply prosocial and want to make a positive difference in others' lives. Work by Stanford psychologist Jamil Zaki has shown that empathizing with and helping others in need seems to be an intuitive response, and dozens of studies, including my own, have found that people often feel happier after conducting acts of kindness. These findings extend earlier research by Stanford professor Frank Flynn and colleagues suggesting that people tend to overestimate how likely their direct request for help would be rejected by others. Finally, other research has even shown that seeking advice can even boost how competent the help-seeker is seen by the advice-giver.

Why is asking for help particularly important?

We love stories about spontaneous help, and that may explain why random acts of kindness go viral on social media. But in reality, the majority of help occurs only after a request has been made. It's often not because people don't want to help and must be pressed to do so. Quite the opposite, people want to help, but they can't help if they don't know someone is suffering or struggling, or what the other person needs and how to help effectively, or whether it is their place to help – perhaps they want to respect others' privacy or agency. A direct request can remove those uncertainties, such that asking for help enables kindness and unlocks opportunities for positive social connections. It can also create emotional closeness when you realize someone trusts you enough to share their vulnerabilities, and by working together toward a shared goal.

It feels like some requests for help may be harder to ask than others. What does research say about different types of help, and how can we use those insights to help us figure out how we should ask for help?

Many factors can influence how difficult it may feel to ask for help. Our recent research has primarily focused on everyday scenarios where the other person is clearly able to help, and all you need is to show up and ask. In some other cases, the kind of help you need may require more specific skills or resources. As long as you make your request Specific, Meaningful, Action-oriented, Realistic, and Time-bound (also known as the SMART criteria), people will likely be happy to help and feel good after helping.

Of course, not all requests have to be specific. When we face mental health challenges, we may have difficulty articulating what kind of help we need. It is okay to reach out to mental health resources and take the time to figure things out together. They are there to help, and they are happy to help.

You mentioned how cultural norms can get in the way of people asking for help. What is one thing we can all do to rethink the role society plays in our lives?

Work on independent and interdependent cultures by Hazel Markus, faculty director of Stanford SPARQ, can shed much light on this issue. Following her insights, I think we can all benefit from having a little bit more interdependency in our micro- and macro-environments. For instance, instead of promoting "self-care" and implying that it is people's own responsibility to sort through their own struggles, perhaps our culture could emphasize the value of caring for each other and create more safe spaces to allow open discussions about our challenges and imperfections.

What inspired your research?

I have always been fascinated by social interaction—how we understand and misunderstand each other's minds, and how social psychology can help people create more positive and meaningful connections. That's why I have studied topics such as giving compliments, discussing disagreement, sharing personal failures, creating inclusive conversations on social media, and translating social and positive psychology research as daily practices for the public. This project is also motivated by that general passion.

But a more immediate trigger of this project is reading scholarly work suggesting that the reason why people underestimate their likelihood of getting help is because they don't recognize how uncomfortable and awkward it would be for someone to say "no" to their request. I agree that people underestimate their chance of getting help upon a direct ask, but based on my personal experience, I saw a different reason—when people ask me for help, I often feel genuinely motivated to help them, more than feeling social pressure and a wish to avoid saying no. This project

Welfare and Social Security Programs

is to voice my different interpretation on why people agree to help. And given that I've seen people who have struggled for too long until it was too late to ask for help, I hope my findings can offer them a bit more comfort when the next time they can really use a helping hand and are debating whether they should ask.

Periodical and Internet Sources Bibliography

The following articles have been selected to supplement the diverse views presented in this chapter.

John Aziz, "Does Welfare Make People Lazy?" the *Week*, January 11, 2015. https://theweek.com/articles/449215/does-welfare-make-people-lazy.

Syed Abul Basher, "Good Intentions, Poor Results: The Problem with Social Safety Net Programmes," the *Daily Star*, October 21, 2020. https://www.thedailystar.net/opinion/news/good-intentions-poor-results-the-problem-social-safety-net-programmes-1981461.

John Blake, "Biden Just Dethroned the Welfare Queen," CNN, May 16, 2021. https://www.cnn.com/2021/05/16/politics/biden-welfare-queen-blake/index.html.

Bruce Covert, "The Myth of the Welfare Queen," the *New Republic*, July 2, 2019. https://newrepublic.com/article/154404/myth-welfare-queen.

Melissa Kearney and Luke Pardue, "Is Cutting the Safety Net an Effective Way to Cut Government Spending?" Econofact, May 24, 2023. https://econofact.org/is-cutting-the-safety-net-an-effective-way-to-reduce-government-spending.

Michael Lind, "The Government Should Keep Its Hands Off Your Medicare," American Compass, October 15, 2021. https://americancompass.org/the-government-should-keep-its-hands-off-your-medicare/.

Jeremy Lybarger, "The Price You Pay," the *Nation*, July 2, 2019. https://www.thenation.com/article/archive/josh-levin-the-queen-book-review/.

Jeff Spross, "Just Give Welfare to Everyone," the *Week*, February 1, 2016. https://theweek.com/articles/601672/just-give-welfare-everyone.

Peter W. Stevenson, "The GOP Push to Cut Unemployment Benefits Is the Welfare Argument All Over Again," the *Washington Post*, May 11, 2021. https://www.washingtonpost.com/politics/2021/05/11/gop-push-cut-unemployment-benefits-is-welfare-argument-all-over-again/.

Welfare and Social Security Programs

Derek Thompson, "Busting the Myth of Welfare Makes People Lazy," the *Atlantic*, March 8, 2018. https://www.theatlantic.com/business/archive/2018/03/welfare-childhood/555119/.

CHAPTER 3

Is the U.S.'s Social Safety Net Better than Other Countries'?

Chapter Preface

How does the United States compare to other countries around the world in terms of its social safety net programs? Worldwide organizations like the International Labor Organization push for mandatory coverage in all countries. They note that more than half of the global population has no access to these lifesaving programs.

It is difficult to comprehend why the United States seems to be behind most other industrialized and economically developed countries when it comes to providing help to disadvantaged people and those experiencing poverty. Previous viewpoints have suggested that there is an underlying "pulling oneself up by the bootstraps" mentality. Or the conservative view that the government should not be responsible for providing help to those who find themselves in need. Or even systemic racism. Why is it then that so many other countries find it appropriate or necessary to take care of their disadvantaged citizens? Do their governments or leaders feel a greater sense of obligation to their citizens? Do working people want to see their taxes going to programs helping others? Do religious convictions or cultural values propel them into action?

The viewpoints in this chapter delve into these questions. Readers will benefit from examining their own beliefs about these ideas after thoughtful and careful reading of the varied viewpoints in this chapter.

VIEWPOINT 1

> *"Universal social protection ensures that anyone who needs social protection can access it at any time. This includes child benefits, pensions for older persons and benefits for people of working age in case of maternity, disability, work injury or for those without jobs."*

All Countries Must Enact Social Protection Networks

The International Labor Organization

In the following viewpoint the International Labor Organization (ILO) maintains that all countries should provide a basic level of social protection. The ILO contends that this is a basic human right, and only benefits the wellbeing of the country in the long run, including economically. The organization contends that poverty is a significant threat to countries around the world, and that many countries lack adequate social protection. However, a handful of countries do have universal social protection, suggesting that it is possible to achieve this. The International Labor Organization is devoted to promoting social justice and internationally recognized human right.

"Countries urged to act on universal social protection," by International Labour Organization (ILO), February 7, 2019. https://www.ilo.org/global/about-the-ilo/newsroom/news/WCMS_669390/lang--en/index.htm. Licensed under CC-BY ND 4.0 International.

Welfare and Social Security Programs

As you read, consider the following questions:
1. According to the viewpoint, what does universal social protection ensure?
2. How much of the global population has no access to social protection measures, according to the ILO?
3. What five areas of national action does the ILO call for in this viewpoint?

Countries have been called on to develop their national social protection systems, which comprise basic, lifelong social security guarantees for all, for health care and income security.*

A call to action to this effect was issued by members of the Global Partnership for Universal Social Protection (USP2030), who convened at a high-level conference at the International Labour Organization (ILO) headquarters on 5 February 2019. The call to action refers to earlier member state commitments, particularly to end poverty, undertaken within the Sustainable Development Agenda.

Universal social protection ensures that anyone who needs social protection can access it at any time. This includes child benefits, pensions for older persons and benefits for people of working age in case of maternity, disability, work injury or for those without jobs.

"The ILO Constitution teaches us that poverty anywhere is a threat to prosperity everywhere. Social protection for anyone in need, at any age, helps ensure against that threat," said Deborah Greenfield, ILO deputy director-general.

Countries in many parts of the world have achieved universal coverage, such as Bolivia, Cabo Verde, Lesotho, Mongolia, Namibia, South Africa and Timor Leste. Mongolia, for instance, has been able to provide universal old age and disability pensions, as well as universal maternity and child benefits.

However, more than half of the global population (4 billion people) still has no access to even one social protection benefit. Forty-five percent of the global population receives only one social protection benefit. Progress has been best in old-age pensions, with 68 percent of older persons receiving a pension. However, child and family benefits are limited to one-third of the world's children: 1.3 billion children do not have social protection. The numbers worsen for persons with disabilities: only 28 percent receive social protection benefits.

"Social protection is an essential tool for reducing poverty and a fundamental human right," said Michelle Bachelet, UN High Commissioner for Human Rights. "Enshrined in the Universal Declaration of Human Rights, this right protects persons in situations of vulnerability, including the elderly, unemployed, sick, injured or living with a disability and those in need of maternity care, so they can retain their fundamental dignity," she added.

In many countries, there are still large coverage gaps and inadequate benefits. One challenge, discussed by meeting participants, is the long-term willingness and capability of governments to invest in the expansion of social protection to all, including informal and gig economy workers and women who may work their whole lives but receive no pension.

"Universal social protection is critical: it raises household incomes, consumption and savings, boosting aggregate demand and enhances people's resilience in the face of shocks, such as those that may result from climate change and structural transformations coming, for example, from new technology affecting work," said Michal Rutkowski, senior Director, Social Protection and Jobs Global Practice, World Bank.

Another challenge is how to secure sustainable and equitable financing for social protection. According to the Organization for Economic Cooperation and Development

(OECD), developing countries spend just 7 percent of GDP on social protection whereas OECD countries spend nearly three times that.

"It's time to make universal social protection a reality. It's sound economic policy," said Isabel Ortiz, ILO director of Social Protection. "To the question about how to finance universal provision," she added, "there is fiscal space to extend social protection even in the poorest countries, some of which have been using a number of alternative options supported by international organizations."

Universal social protection is achieved through national policies and programmes that provide equitable access to all people and protect them throughout their lives against poverty and risks to their livelihoods and well-being. This protection can be provided through a range of mechanisms, including via cash or in-kind benefits, contributory or non-contributory schemes, and programmes to enhance human capital, productive assets and access to jobs. The provision of a social protection floor for all people in developing countries costs as little as 1.6 percent of their gross domestic product (GDP) on average.

"There is a strong business case for social protection. We need to invest in it for development to occur and not wait for development to put it in place. Additional finance can be provided by the private sector, cash transfers and governments who fight tax evasion and avoidance," said Gabriela Ramos, chief of staff and G20 Sherpa, OECD.

National action is required in five areas: protection throughout the life cycle; universal coverage; country-level ownership; sustainable and equitable financing, both domestic and international; and participation and social dialogue.

The Global Partnership for Universal Social Protection (USP2030) supports countries, accelerating progress in building their social protection systems. All countries are invited to join the partnership.

Notes

* 'Social protection floor' is the term used to describe nationally defined sets of basic social security guarantees that should ensure, as a minimum that, over the life cycle, all in need have access to essential health care and to basic income security which together secure effective access to goods and services defined as necessary at the national level.

VIEWPOINT 2

"Using surveys and other standardized data on quality and health care outcomes to measure and compare patient and physician experiences across a group of 11 high-income nations, the researchers rank the United States last overall in providing equitably accessible, affordable, high-quality health care."

The United States Has a Poor Health Care System Compared to Other Countries
Eric C. Schneider

In the following viewpoint Eric C. Schneider asserts that the United States does an abysmal job of providing health care for its citizens compared to many other countries. Schneider provides statistics and evidence to support his claims. The data suggests that income is more important to getting quality essential health care in the United States than in other countries, and that even high-income people in the United States are likely to experience financial barriers to care. Finally, Schneider offers a plan for how the United States could do a better job of providing equitable health outcomes for all its citizens. Eric C. Schneider is executive vice president of the Quality Measurement and Research Group of the National Committee for Quality Assurance.

"New International Study: U.S. Health System Ranks Last Among 11 Countries; Many Americans Struggle to Afford Care as Income Inequality Widens," by Eric C. Schneider, The Commonwealth Fund, August 4, 2021. Reprinted by permission.

Is the U.S.'s Social Safety Net Better than Other Countries'?

As you read, consider the following questions:
1. According to this viewpoint, can Americans afford health care as easily as people living in many other countries?
2. How does the United States do on health care outcomes, according to data cited by the author?
3. What are two things the United States can and should do to increase its health care ranking, according to Schneider?

The U.S. health system trails far behind a number of other high-income countries when it comes to affordability, administrative efficiency, equity, and health care outcomes, according to a new Commonwealth Fund study. Using surveys and other standardized data on quality and health care outcomes to measure and compare patient and physician experiences across a group of 11 high-income nations, the researchers rank the United States last overall in providing equitably accessible, affordable, high-quality health care.

The report, *Mirror, Mirror 2021—Reflecting Poorly: Health Care in the U.S. Compared to Other High-Income Countries,* shows that getting good, essential health care in the United States depends on income—more so than in any other wealthy country. Since 2004, the United States has ranked last in every edition of the report, falling further behind on some indicators, despite spending the most on health care.

Half (50%) of lower-income U.S. adults reported that costs prevented them from getting needed health care, compared to a quarter (27%) of higher-income adults. In the United Kingdom, only 12 percent of people with lower incomes and 7 percent with higher incomes reported financial barriers to care.

Remarkably, a high-income person in the United States was more likely to report financial barriers than a low-income person in nearly all the other countries surveyed: Australia, Canada,

France, Germany, the Netherlands, New Zealand, Norway, Sweden, Switzerland, and the U.K.

Norway, the Netherlands, and Australia were the top performers overall. In the middle of the pack were the U.K., Germany, New Zealand, Sweden, and France. Switzerland and Canada ranked lower than those countries, although both still performed much better than the United States.

Among the 11 nations surveyed, the United States is the only one without universal health insurance coverage. Other research suggests that the United States spends less than other high-income countries on social services, such as child care, education, paid sick leave, and unemployment insurance, which could improve population health.

Additional report findings related to the United States include:

- Access to Care: Compared to people in other high-income countries, Americans of all incomes have the hardest time affording the health care they need. The United States ranks last on most measures of financial barriers to care, with 38 percent of adults reporting they did not receive recommended medical care in the past year because of cost. This is more than four times the rates for people in Norway (8%) and the Netherlands (9%). U.S. adults were also much more likely to report that their insurance denied payment of a claim or paid less than expected. Thirty-four percent of U.S. adults reported this, compared to 4 percent of adults in Germany and the U.K.
- Care Process: The United States ranks near the top, in second place, for care process, which combines four categories of indicators: preventive care, safe care, coordinated care, and patient engagement and preferences. Along with the U.K. and Sweden, on average the United States achieves higher performance on preventive care, which includes rates of mammography screening and influenza vaccination for older adults as well as the percentage of adults who talked with a health care provider about nutrition, smoking, and

alcohol use. The United States also ranks high on safe care and patient engagement. However, not all American adults have equitable access to care and because the United States was ranked last in the other domains, including health care outcomes, it still ranks last overall.
- Health Care Outcomes: The United States ranks at the bottom on health care outcomes. Compared to other countries, the United States performs poorly on maternal mortality, infant mortality, life expectancy at age 60, and deaths that were potentially preventable with timely access to effective health care. The U.S. rate of preventable mortality (177 deaths per 100,000 population) was more than double that of the best-performing country, Switzerland (83 deaths per 100,000).
- Administrative Efficiency: The United States ranks last in administrative efficiency because of how much time providers and patients spend dealing with paperwork, duplicative medical testing, and insurance disputes. Nearly two-thirds (63%) of U.S. primary care doctors reported the time spent trying to get their patients needed treatment because of insurance coverage restrictions was a major problem. In Norway, which ranks first on this measure, only 7 percent of doctors reported this problem.

Moving Forward

The authors say there are a number of lessons for the United States that could inform efforts to attain better and more equitable health outcomes:

- Expand health insurance coverage. The highest-performing countries have universal coverage and consumer protections, so people can get the health care they need at little or no cost.
- Strengthen primary care. Affordable, timely, and convenient primary care, available on nights and weekends in all communities, keeps people healthier and lowers costs in the long run.

- Reduce administrative burden. Reducing the paperwork and administrative complexity in the U.S. health care system would give countless hours back to patients, caregivers, and physicians while making the system easier for people to navigate.
- Invest more in social services. Factors beyond traditional health care, such as housing, education, nutrition, and transportation, have a substantial effect on people's health. Investing in services that provide support in these areas can improve population health and reduce health care costs.

How We Conducted This Study

The 2021 edition of *Mirror, Mirror* was constructed using the same methodological framework developed in consultation with an expert advisory committee for the 2017 report.[1] Another expert advisory panel was convened to review the data, measures, and methods used in the 2021 edition.[2]

Using data available from Commonwealth Fund international surveys of the public and physicians and other sources of standardized data on quality and health care outcomes, and with the guidance of the independent expert advisory panel, the authors selected 71 measures relevant to health care system performance, organizing them into five performance domains: access, care process, administrative efficiency, equity, and health care outcomes. The criteria for selecting measures and grouping within domains included: importance of the measure, standardization of the measure and data across the countries, salience to policymakers, relevance to performance improvement efforts. *Mirror, Mirror* is unique in its inclusion of survey measures designed to reflect the perspectives of patients and professionals—the people who experience health care in each country during the course of a year. Nearly three-quarters of the measures come from surveys designed to elicit the experiences of the public and primary care professionals with their health system.

The method for calculating performance scores and rankings is similar to that used in the 2017 report, except that the authors modified the calculation of mean performance scores to address the outlier status of the United States on several measures.

For each measure, the authors converted each country's result (e.g., the percentage of survey respondents giving a certain response or a mortality rate) to a measure-specific, "normalized" performance score. This score was calculated as the difference between the country result and the group mean (after excluding the U.S. as described below), divided by the standard deviation of the results for each measure. Normalizing the results based on the standard deviation accounts for differences between measures in the range of variation among country-specific results. A positive performance score indicates the country performs above the group average; a negative score indicates the country performs below the group average. Performance scores in the equity domain were based on the difference between the two income groups, with a wider difference interpreted as a measure of lower equity between the two income strata in each country.

For each performance domain, the authors calculated a mean performance score for each country based on the performance measures in the domain. A standard statistical approach identified the U.S. as an extreme outlier on some measures in several domains or subdomains (*affordability, preventive care, equity,* and *health care outcomes*). To avoid outlier bias and for consistency, the U.S. was excluded from the calculation of the mean domain and overall performance scores. Then each country was ranked from 1 to 11 based on the mean domain performance score, with 1 representing the highest performance score and 11 representing the lowest performance score.

The overall performance score for each country was calculated as the mean of the five domain-specific performance scores. Then, each country was ranked from 1 to 11 based on this summary mean score, again with 1 representing the highest overall performance score and rank 11 representing the lowest overall performance score.

Welfare and Social Security Programs

Notes

1. Eric C. Schneider et al., Mirror, Mirror 2017: International Comparison Reflects Flaws and Opportunities for Better U.S. Health Care (Commonwealth Fund, July 2017).
2. Members of the 2021 advisory panel include: Marc Elliott, M.A., Ph.D., Distinguished Chair in Statistics and Senior Principal Researcher, RAND Corporation; Niek Klazinga, M.D., Ph.D., Head of the Health Care Quality Indicators (HCQI) Project, Organisation for Economic Co-operation and Development Health Division; Jennifer Nuzzo, Dr.PH., Senior Scholar, Johns Hopkins Center for Health Security; Irene Papanicolas, Ph.D, Associate Professor of Health Economics, Department of Health Policy, London School of Economics and Political Science.

VIEWPOINT 3

> *"The United States remains one of the only advanced industrialized democracies in the world without universal coverage."*

There Are Various Reasons Why the United States Resists Universal Health Coverage

Timothy Callaghan

In the following viewpoint Timothy Callaghan examines why the United States doesn't have a system of national health care as part of its public assistance programs, especially considering health care spending is high in the country. Callaghan details the reasons why the United States is different than most developed countries in this respect. The United States's unique culture plays a major part in this, according to Callaghan, though he also notes the difficulty in enacting entitlement programs. Timothy Callaghan is an assistant professor at Texas A&M University in the health sciences department.

As you read, consider the following questions:

1. Does the Affordable Care Act (ACA) count as universal health coverage, according to Callaghan?
2. What are the three negative health care outcomes in the United States mentioned in this viewpoint?

"Three reasons the US doesn't have universal health coverage," by Timothy Callaghan, The Conversation, October 26, 2016. https://theconversation.com/three-reasons-the-us-doesnt-have-universal-health-coverage-67292. Licensed under CC-BY ND 4.0 International.

3. According to Callaghan, do most Americans want universal health coverage?

Amidst the partisan rancor and the unusual tilt toward questions on civility during the second and third presidential debates, Hillary Clinton and Donald Trump drew the attention of health experts when they articulated their path forward for health policy in America.

Responding to questions about the lack of affordability in the Affordable Care Act, the candidates detailed how they would address the increasingly glaring flaws in President [Barack] Obama's signature policy achievement. Mr. Trump, who called the ACA a "disaster," has pushed for repeal of the law. He wants to replace it with block grants for Medicaid and the sale of health insurance across state lines.

Secretary Clinton has emphasized the positive aspects of the ACA, including safeguards to ensure that insurers cannot deny coverage because of an applicant's preexisting conditions. She has argued that changes must be made at the edges of the existing law.

As important as these discussions have been for providing the American public details about each candidate's future plans in the health policy arena, they were also significant for the option they ignored—the possibility of universal health coverage in America.

The ACA certainly brought us closer to universal coverage, a system where the government typically pays for basic health care services for everyone. However, the fact that a true national health insurance system didn't even warrant discussion by the major party candidates is surprising—or at least should be. The United States remains one of the only advanced industrialized democracies in the world without universal coverage.

While this in and of itself is not a problem, the United States also spends more on health care as a percentage of GDP than any other advanced country in the world and has worse health outcomes—with lower life expectancy, higher infant mortality and higher obesity rates than comparable countries like Australia, Canada, the United Kingdom, Germany, France and Japan.

It is also surprising because Bernie Sanders, running on a platform that included universal coverage or what he called Medicare for all, generated massive grassroots support and energized the millennial population that makes up an increasing percentage of the electorate.

Given these facts, it is important to ask: Why isn't universal coverage through a national health insurance system even being considered in America? Research in health policy points to three explanations.

No. 1: We Don't Want It

One key reason is the unique political culture in America. As a nation that began on the back of immigrants with an entrepreneurial spirit and without a feudal system to ingrain a rigid social structure, Americans are more likely to be individualistic.

In other words, Americans, and conservatives in particular, have a strong belief in classical liberalism and the idea that the government should play a limited role in society. Given that universal coverage inherently clashes with this belief in individualism and limited government, it is perhaps not surprising that it has never been enacted in America even as it has been enacted elsewhere.

Public opinion certainly supports this idea. Survey research conducted by the International Social Survey Program has found that a lower percentage of Americans believe health care for the sick is a government responsibility than individuals in other advanced countries like Canada, the U.K., Germany or Sweden.

The Big Picture

Could the poorer overall health of the U.S. population be the result of fewer funds allocated to assist young and working-age people? The authors believe this low level of spending, combined with relatively high U.S. poverty rates, could be leading to an

Social Spending in the United States

There is speculation that many poor health outcomes in the United States are related in part to inattention to social factors like housing, nutrition, and education. But according to the Commonwealth Fund's Roosa Tikkanen and Eric Schneider, M.D., the United States—despite high levels of spending devoted to health care—spends a similar percentage of its gross domestic product on social programs as other high-income countries do.

Writing in the *New England Journal of Medicine,* the researchers suggest that the way the United States spends these funds is limiting their impact. The authors used 2015 data from the Organization for Economic Cooperation and Development to compare what the United States devotes to social spending against the average for 27 high-income European countries.

What the Study Found

Despite spending roughly the same per person, the United States spent less to support the social needs of younger and working-age populations than did other countries. Per person spending on benefits like early childhood education and parental leave in the United States was about one-third of what other countries spent—$360 vs. $1,107.

- The United States spent about one-quarter the amount on unemployment benefits for working-age adults as did the other countries ($111 vs. $428). Unemployment benefits in the United States replace 6 percent of lost income, compared with an average of 33 percent abroad.
- The United States is an outlier in the other direction in the amount it allocates to older populations. The United States spent $6,522 per capita on benefits like pensions, home help, and residential services compared with an average $4,268 in the other countries.

"Does the United States Allocate Its Social Spending Dollars Wisely?," by Roosa Tikkanen and Eric C. Schneider, The Commonwealth Fund, March 5, 2020.

accumulation of unmet needs and worse health later in life. Meanwhile, higher U.S. spending on its older populations may be "'too little, too late' to reverse preventable health problems incurred at earlier ages," the authors conclude.

The Bottom Line
The United States and other high-income countries spend similar amounts on programs to support people's social needs. But the U.S. spending mix is different, with more allocated to older populations and less to young and working-age people. This difference could help explain the country's poorer health outcomes.

No. 2: Interest Groups Don't Want It
Even as American political culture helps to explain the health care debate in America, culture is far from the only reason America lacks universal coverage. Another factor that has limited debate about national health insurance is the role of interest groups in influencing the political process. The legislative battle over the content of the ACA, for example, generated US$1.2 billion in lobbying in 2009 alone.

The insurance industry was a key player in this process, spending over $100 million to help shape the ACA and keep private insurers, as opposed to the government, as the key cog in American health care.

Recent reports suggest that lobbyists are already preparing to fight a potential "public option" under the ACA. Should any attempt at comprehensive national health insurance ever be made, lobbyists would certainly mobilize to prevent its implementation.

No. 3: Entitlement Programs Are Hard in General to Enact
A third reason America lacks universal health coverage and the 2016 candidates have avoided the topic altogether is that America's political institutions make it difficult for massive entitlement programs to be enacted. As policy experts have pointed out in

studies of the U.S. health system, the country doesn't "have a comprehensive national health insurance system because American political institutions are structurally biased against this kind of comprehensive reform."

The political system is prone to inertia and any attempt at comprehensive reform must pass through the obstacle course of congressional committees, budget estimates, conference committees, amendments and a potential veto while opponents of reform publicly bash the bill.

Ultimately, the United States remains one of the only advanced industrialized nations without a comprehensive national health insurance system and with little prospect for one developing under the next president because of the many ways America is exceptional.

Its culture is unusually individualistic, favoring personal over government responsibility; lobbyists are particularly active, spending billions to ensure that private insurers maintain their status in the health system; and our institutions are designed in a manner that limits major social policy changes from happening. As long as these facts remain, there is little reason to expect universal coverage in America anytime soon, regardless of who becomes president.

VIEWPOINT 4

> "A growing body of evidence suggests that social services play an important role in shaping health trajectories and mitigating health disparities."

France, Denmark, Norway, and Sweden Spend More than the United States on Social Programs

David Squires and Chloe Anderson

In this viewpoint David Squires and Chloe Anderson report on the comparison of health care spending, health care visits, use of sophisticated medical equipment, use of and spending on prescription drugs, and other aspects of health care between the United States and other countries around the world. The authors point out that even with greater spending, the United States lags behind many countries in almost all areas of health care except for specialized cancer care. Surprisingly, they also note that public health care spending is high in the United States even though many people aren't covered by it. David Squires and Chloe Anderson are former researchers for the Commonwealth Fund.

As you read, consider the following questions:

1. How does personal spending on health care in the United States compare to other countries?

"U.S. Health Care from a Global Perspective," by David Squires and Chloe Anderson, The Commonwealth Fund, October 8, 2015. Reprinted by permission.

2. How does the use of medical technology in the United States compare to other countries? How does the use of prescription drugs in the United States compare?
3. What do the authors use as evidence suggesting the United States has poor population health?

This analysis draws upon data from the Organization for Economic Cooperation and Development and other cross-national analyses to compare health care spending, supply, utilization, prices, and health outcomes across 13 high-income countries: Australia, Canada, Denmark, France, Germany, Japan, Netherlands, New Zealand, Norway, Sweden, Switzerland, the United Kingdom, and the United States. These data predate the major insurance provisions of the Affordable Care Act. In 2013, the United States spent far more on health care than these other countries. Higher spending appeared to be largely driven by greater use of medical technology and higher health care prices, rather than more frequent doctor visits or hospital admissions. In contrast, U.S. spending on social services made up a relatively small share of the economy relative to other countries. Despite spending more on health care, Americans had poor health outcomes, including shorter life expectancy and greater prevalence of chronic conditions.

Overview

Cross-national comparisons allow us to track the performance of the U.S. health care system, highlight areas of strength and weakness, and identify factors that may impede or accelerate improvement. This analysis is the latest in a series of Commonwealth Fund cross-national comparisons that use health data from the Organization for Economic Cooperation and Development (OECD), as well as from other sources, to assess U.S. health care system spending, supply, utilization, and prices relative to other countries, as well as a limited set of health outcomes.[1,2] Thirteen high-income countries are included: Australia, Canada, Denmark, France, Germany, Japan, Netherlands, New Zealand, Norway, Sweden, Switzerland, the United Kingdom, and the United States. On measures where data are widely available, the value for the median OECD country is also shown. Almost all data are for years prior to the major insurance provisions of the Affordable Care Act; most are for 2013.

Health care spending in the United States far exceeds that of other high-income countries, though spending growth has slowed in the United States and in most other countries in recent years.[3] Even though the United States is the only country without a publicly financed universal health system, it still spends more public dollars on health care than all but two of the other countries. Americans have relatively few hospital admissions and physician visits, but are greater users of expensive technologies like magnetic resonance imaging (MRI) machines. Available cross-national pricing data suggest that prices for health care are notably higher in the United States, potentially explaining a large part of the higher health spending. In contrast, the United States devotes a relatively small share of its economy to social services, such as housing assistance, employment programs, disability benefits, and food security.[4] Finally, despite its heavy investment in health care, the United States sees poorer results on several key health outcome measures such as life expectancy and the prevalence of chronic conditions. Mortality rates from cancer are low and have fallen more quickly in the United States than in other countries, but the reverse is true for mortality from ischemic heart disease.

Key Findings

The United States Is the Highest Spender on Health Care

Data from the OECD show that the United States spent 17.1 percent of its gross domestic product (GDP) on health care in 2013. This was almost 50 percent more than the next-highest spender (France, 11.6% of GDP) and almost double what was spent in the U.K.

(8.8%). U.S. spending per person was equivalent to $9,086 (not adjusted for inflation).

Since 2009, health care spending growth has slowed in the United States and most other countries. The real growth rate per capita in the United States declined from 2.47 percent between 2003 and 2009 to 1.50 percent between 2009 and 2013. In Denmark and the United Kingdom, the growth rate actually became negative. The timing and cross-national nature of the slowdown suggest a connection to the 2007–2009 global financial crisis and its aftereffects, though additional factors also may be at play.[5]

Private Spending on Health Care Is Highest in the United States

In 2013, the average U.S. resident spent $1,074 out-of-pocket on health care, for things like copayments for doctor's office visits and prescription drugs and health insurance deductibles. Only the Swiss spent more at $1,630, while France and the Netherlands spent less than one-fourth as much ($277 and $270, respectively). As for other private health spending, including on private insurance premiums, U.S. spending towered over that of the other countries at $3,442 per capita—more than five times what was spent in Canada ($654), the second-highest spending country.[6]

U.S. Public Spending on Health Care Is High, Despite Covering Fewer Residents

Public spending on health care amounted to $4,197 per capita in the United States in 2013, more than in any other country except Norway ($4,981) and the Netherlands ($4,495), despite the fact that the United States was the only country studied that did not have a universal health care system. In the United States, about 34 percent of residents were covered by public programs in 2013, including Medicare and Medicaid.[7] By comparison, every resident in the United Kingdom is covered by the public system and spending was $2,802 per capita. Public spending on health care would be even greater in the United States if the tax exclusion for employer-sponsored health insurance (amounting to about $250 billion each year) was counted as a public expenditure.[8]

Despite Spending More on Health Care, Americans Have Fewer Hospital and Physician Visits

The United States had fewer practicing physicians in 2013 than in the median OECD country (2.6 versus 3.2 physicians per 1,000 population). With only four per year, Americans also had fewer physician visits than the OECD median (6.5 visits). In contrast, the average Canadian had 7.7 physician visits and the average Japanese resident had 12.9 visits in 2012.

In the United States, there were also fewer hospital beds and fewer discharges per capita than in the median OECD country.

Americans Appear to Be Greater Consumers of Medical Technology, Including Diagnostic Imaging and Pharmaceuticals

The United States stood out as a top consumer of sophisticated diagnostic imaging technology. Americans had the highest per capita rates of MRI, computed tomography (CT), and positron emission tomography (PET) exams among the countries where data were available. The United States and Japan were among the countries with the highest number of these imaging machines.[9]

In addition, Americans were top consumers of prescription drugs. Based on findings from the 2013 Commonwealth Fund International Surveys, adults in the United States and New Zealand on average take more prescription drugs (2.2 per adult) than adults in other countries.

Health Care Prices Are Higher in the United States Compared with Other Countries

Data published by the International Federation of Health Plans suggest that hospital and physician prices for procedures were highest in the United States in 2013.[10] The average price of bypass surgery was $75,345 in the United States. This is more than

$30,000 higher than in the second-highest country, Australia, where the procedure costs $42,130. According to the same data source, MRI and CT scans were also most expensive in the United States. While these pricing data are subject to significant methodological limitations, they illustrate a pattern of significantly higher prices in many areas of U.S. health care.

Other studies have observed high U.S. prices for pharmaceuticals. A 2013 investigation by Kanavos and colleagues created a cross-national price index for a basket of widely used in-patent pharmaceuticals. In 2010, all countries studied had lower prices than the United States. In Australia, Canada, and the United Kingdom, prices were about 50 percent lower.[11]

The U.S. Invests the Smallest Share of Its Economy on Social Services

A 2013 study by Bradley and Taylor found that the United States spent the least on social services—such as retirement and disability benefits, employment programs, and supportive housing—among the countries studied in this report, at just 9 percent of GDP.[12] Canada, Australia and New Zealand had similarly low rates of spending, while France, Sweden, Switzerland, and Germany devoted roughly twice as large a share of their economy to social services as did the United States.

The United States was also the only country studied where health care spending accounted for a greater share of GDP than social services spending. In aggregate, U.S. health and social services spending rank near the middle of the pack.

Despite Its High Spending on Health Care, the United States Has Poor Population Health

On several measures of population health, Americans had worse outcomes than their international peers. The United States had the lowest life expectancy at birth of the countries studied, at 78.8 years in 2013, compared with the OECD median of 81.2 years. Additionally, the United States had the highest infant mortality rate among the countries studied, at 6.1 deaths per 1,000 live births in 2011; the rate in the OECD median country was 3.5 deaths.

The prevalence of chronic diseases also appeared to be higher in the United States. The 2014 Commonwealth Fund International Health Policy Survey found that 68 percent of U.S. adults age 65 or older had at least two chronic conditions. In other countries, this figure ranged from 33 percent (U.K.) to 56 percent (Canada).[13]

A 2013 report from the Institute of Medicine reviewed the literature about the health disadvantages of Americans relative to residents of other high-income countries. It found the United States performed poorly on several important determinants of health.[14] More than a third of adults in the United States were obese in 2012, a rate that was about 15 percent higher than the next-highest country, New Zealand. The United States had one of the lowest smoking rates in 2013, but one of the highest rates of tobacco consumption in the 1960s and 1970s. This earlier period of heavy tobacco use may still be contributing to relatively worse health outcomes among older U.S. adults.[15] Other potential contributors to the United States' health disadvantage include the large number of uninsured, as well as differences in lifestyle, environment, and rates of accidents and violence.

The Institute of Medicine found that poorer health in the United States was not simply the result of economic, social, or racial and ethnic disadvantages—even well-off, nonsmoking, nonobese Americans appear in worse health than their counterparts abroad.

The United States Performs Well on Cancer Care but Has High Rates of Mortality from Heart Disease and Amputations as a Result of Diabetes

One area where the United States appeared to have comparatively good health outcomes was cancer care. A 2015 study by Stevens et al. found that mortality rates from cancer in the United States were lower and had declined faster between 1995 and 2007 than in most industrialized countries.[16] Other research based on survival rates also suggests that U.S. cancer care is above average, though these studies are disputed on methodological grounds.[17]

The opposite trend appears for ischemic heart disease, where the United States had among the highest mortality rates in 2013—128 per 100,000 population compared with 95 in the median OECD country. Since 1995, mortality rates have fallen significantly in all countries as a result of improved treatment and changes in risk factors.[18] However, this decline was less pronounced in the United States, where rates declined from 225 to 128 deaths per 100,000 population—considerably less than countries like Denmark, where rates declined from 242 to 71 deaths per 100,000 population.

The United States also had high rates of adverse outcomes from diabetes, with 17.1 lower extremity amputations per 100,000 population in 2011. Rates in Sweden, Australia and the U.K. were less than one-third as high.

Discussion

Health care spending in the United States far exceeds that in other countries, despite a global slowdown in spending growth in recent years. At 17.1 percent of GDP, the United States devotes at least 50 percent more of its economy to health care than do other countries. Even public spending on health care, on a per capita basis, is higher in the United States than in most other countries with universal public coverage.

How can we explain the higher U.S. spending? In line with previous studies,[19] the results of this analysis suggest that the excess is likely driven by greater utilization of medical technology and higher prices, rather than use of routine services, such as more frequent visits to physicians and hospitals.

High health care spending has far-reaching consequences in the U.S. economy, contributing to wage stagnation, personal bankruptcy, and budget deficits, and creating a competitive disadvantage relative to other nations.[20] One potential consequence of high health spending is that it may crowd out other forms of social spending that support health. In the United States, health care spending substantially outweighs spending on social services. This imbalance may contribute to the country's poor health outcomes. A growing body of evidence suggests that social services play an important role in shaping health trajectories and mitigating health disparities.[21,22] Additional cross-national research is needed to better understand the relationship between social services and health, as well as other health determinants like lifestyle and environment.

New care models that reward health care providers based on their patient population's health outcomes (e.g., accountable care organizations) are an interesting development. Such accountability could create a business case for health care providers to invest in certain social services or other nonclinical interventions, if doing so would be a cost-effective way to improve patients' health.[23] Over the long term, such a strategy could potentially alter the current balance between health and social services spending.

Notes

[1] D. Squires, "The Global Slowdown in Health Care Spending," *Journal of the American Medical Association,* Aug. 6, 2014 312(5):485–86; D. Squires, *Explaining High Health Care Spending in the United States: An International Comparison of Supply, Utilization, Prices, and Quality* (New York: The Commonwealth Fund, May 2012); D. Squires, *The U.S. Health System in Perspective: A Comparison of Twelve Industrialized Nations* (New York: The Commonwealth Fund, July 2011); G. F. Anderson and D. Squires, *Measuring the U.S. Health Care System: A Cross-National Comparison* (New York: The Commonwealth Fund, June 2010); G. F. Anderson and B. K. Frogner, "Health Spending in OECD Countries: Obtaining Value per Dollar," *Health Affairs,* Nov./Dec. 2008 27(6):1718–27; G. F. Anderson, B. K. Frogner, and U. E. Reinhardt, "Health Spending in OECD Countries in 2004: An Update," *Health Affairs,* Sept./Oct. 2007 26(5):1481–89; G. F. Anderson, P. S. Hussey, B. K. Frogner et al., "Health Spending in the United States and the Rest of the Industrialized World," *Health Affairs,* July/Aug. 2005 24(4):903–14; U. E. Reinhardt, P. S. Hussey, and G. F. Anderson, "U.S. Health Care Spending in an International Context," *Health Affairs,* May/June 2004 23(3):10–25; G. F. Anderson, U. E. Reinhardt, P. S. Hussey et al., "It's the Prices, Stupid: Why the United States Is So Different from Other Countries," *Health Affairs,* May/June 2003, 22(3):89–105; U. E. Reinhardt, P. S. Hussey, and G. F. Anderson, "Cross-National Comparisons of Health Systems Using OECD Data, 1999," *Health Affairs,* May/ June 2002 21(3):169–81; G. F. Anderson and P. S. Hussey, "Comparing Health System Performance in OECD Countries," *Health Affairs,* May/June 2001 20(3):219–32; G. F. Anderson, J. Hurst, P. S. Hussey et al., "Health Spending and Outcomes: Trends in OECD Countries, 1960–

1998," *Health Affairs,* May/June 2000 19(3):150–57; and G. F. Anderson and J. P. Poullier, "Health Spending, Access, and Outcomes: Trends in Industrialized Countries," *Health Affairs,* May/June 1999 18(3):178–92.

[2] Unlike the Fund's Mirror, Mirror on the Wall series, this report does not attempt to assess overall health system performance, or rank health systems across various metrics. See: K. Davis, K. Stremikis, C. Schoen, and D. Squires, *Mirror, Mirror on the Wall, 2014 Update: How the U.S. Health Care System Compares Internationally* (New York: The Commonwealth Fund, June 2014).

[3] Organization for Economic Cooperation and Development, *OECD Health Data 2015*(Paris: OECD, June 2015).

[4] E. H. Bradley and L. A. Taylor, *The American Health Care Paradox: Why Spending More Is Getting Us Less* (New York: Public Affairs, 2013).

[5] Squires, "Global Slowdown," 2014.

[6] Because of data limitations in several countries, the breakdown of health spending by source of financing is for current spending only, meaning it excludes capital formation of health care providers. In most countries, those amounts range between 2 percent and 7 percent of total health spending.

[7] U.S. Census Bureau, *Health Insurance in the United States: 2013—Tables & Figures,* 2014.

[8] Congressional Budget Office, *Options for Reducing The Deficit: 2014 to 2023*(Washington, D.C.: CBO, Nov. 2013).

[9] It should be noted that, despite the comparatively high levels of use in the U.S., growth in medical imaging appears to have leveled off in recent years after surging through much of the 2000s. The slowdown has been attributed to patient cost-sharing, prior authorization, best-practice guidelines, and other strategies to reduce potentially unnecessary utilization. See D. W. Lee and F. Levy, "The Sharp Slowdown in Growth of Medical Imaging: An Early Analysis Suggests Combination of Policies Was the Cause," *Health Affairs,* Aug. 2012 31(8):1876–84.

[10] International Federation of Health Plans, 2013 Comparative Price Report.

[11] P. Kanavos, A. Ferrario, S. Vandoros et al., "Higher U.S. Branded Drug Prices and Spending Compared to Other Countries May Stem Partly from Quick Uptake of New Drugs," *Health Affairs,* April 2013 32(4):753–61.

[12] Bradley and Taylor, *American Health Care Paradox,* 2013.

[13] Chronic conditions included hypertension or high blood pressure, heart disease, diabetes, lung problems, mental health problems, cancer, and joint pain/arthritis. See Commonwealth Fund 2014 International Health Policy Survey of Older Adults.

[14] J. D. Freeman, S. Kadiyala, J. F. Bell et al., "The Causal Effect of Health Insurance on Utilization and Outcomes in Adults: A Systematic Review of US Studies," *Medical Care,* 2008 46(10):1023–32; and S. H. Woolf and L. Aron (eds.), *U.S. Health in International Perspective: Shorter Lives, Poorer Health* (Washington, D.C.: National Academies Press, 2013).

[15] Woolf and Aron (eds.), *U.S. Health in International Perspective,* 2013.

[16] W. Stevens, T. J. Philipson, Z. M. Khan et al., "Cancer Mortality Reductions Were Greatest Among Countries Where Cancer Care Spending Rose the Most, 1995–2007," *Health Affairs,* April 2015 34(4):562–70.

[17] T. Philipson, M. Eber, D. N. Lakdawalla et al., "An Analysis of Whether Higher Health Care Spending in the United States Versus Europe Is 'Worth It' in the Case of Cancer," *Health Affairs,* April 2012 31(4):667–75; S. Soneji and J. Yang, "New Analysis Reexamines the Value of Cancer Care in the United States Compared to Western Europe," *Health Affairs,* March 2015 34(3):390–97; D. Goldman,

D. Lakdawalla, and T. Philipson, "Mortality Versus Survival in International Comparisons of Cancer Care," *Health Affairs Blog,* March 20, 2015; and H. G. Welch and E. Fisher, "Revisiting Mortality Versus Survival in International Comparisons of Cancer Care," *Health Affairs Blog,* April 1, 2015.

[18] Organization for Economic Cooperation and Development, *Cardiovascular Disease and Diabetes: Policies for Better Health and Quality of Care* (Paris: OECD, June 2015).

[19] Squires, *Explaining High Health Care Spending,* 2012; Anderson, Frogner, and Reinhardt, "Health Spending in OECD Countries," 2007; M. J. Laugesen and S. A. Glied, "Higher Fees Paid to U.S. Physicians Drive Higher Spending for Physician Services Compared to Other Countries," *Health Affairs,* Sept. 2011 30(9):1647–56.

[20] D. I. Auerbach and A. L. Kellermann, "A Decade of Health Care Cost Growth Has Wiped Out Real Income Gains for an Average U.S. Family," *Health Affairs,* Sept. 2011 30(9):1630–36; D. Blumenthal and D. Squires, "Do Health Care Costs Fuel Economic Inequality in the United States?" *The Commonwealth Fund Blog,* Sept. 9, 2014; D. U. Himmelstein, D. Thorne, E. Warren et al., "Medical Bankruptcy in the United States, 2007: Results of a National Study," *American Journal of Medicine,* Aug. 2009 122(8):741–46; RAND Health, *How Does Growth in Health Care Costs Affect the American Family?* (Santa Monica, Calif.: RAND, 2011); and T. Johnson, *Healthcare Costs and U.S. Competitiveness* (New York: Council on Foreign Relations, March 2012).

[21] M. Avendano and I. Kawachi, "Why Do Americans Have Shorter Life Expectancy and Worse Health Than Do People in Other High-Income Countries?" *Annual Review of Public Health,* March 2014 35:307–25; and Bradley and Taylor, *American Health Care Paradox,* 2013.

[22] E. H. Bradley, B. R. Elkins, J. Herrin et al., "Health and Social Services Expenditures: Associations with Health Outcomes," *BMJ Quality & Safety,* published online March 29, 2011.

[23] D. Bachrach, H. Pfister, K. Wallis et al., *Addressing Patients' Social Needs: An Emerging Business Case for Provider Investment* (New York: The Commonwealth Fund, May 2014).

Periodical and Internet Sources Bibliography

The following articles have been selected to supplement the diverse views presented in this chapter.

Nicolo Bird, "Expanding and Improving Social Safety Nets Through Digitalization: Conceptual Framework and Review of Country Experiences," International Monetary Fund, December 7, 2023. https://www.imf.org/en/Publications/IMF-Notes/Issues/2023/12/07/Expanding-and-Improving-Social-Safety-Nets-Through-Digitalization-Conceptual-Framework-and-541091.

Liana Brinded, "Top 10 Countries for Best Social Safety Nets to Battle COVID-19 Are All in Europe," Yahoo Finance UK, December 21, 2020. https://uk.finance.yahoo.com/news/davos-wef-global-competitiveness-report-special-edition-2020-recovery-country-ranking-social-safety-nets-090738867.html.

Katharina Buchholz, "These Countries Spend the Most, and the Least, On Social Benefits," World Economic Forum, February 10, 2021. https://www.weforum.org/agenda/2021/02/social-spending-highest-lowest-country-comparison-oecd-france-economics-politics-welfare/.

Daniel Bunn, Sean Bray, and Joost Haddinga, "Insights into the Tax Systems of Scandinavian Countries," Tax Foundation, April 20, 2023. https://taxfoundation.org/blog/scandinavian-social-programs-taxes-2023/.

Joseph de Weck, "France's Welfare State Kept Macron in Power," *Internationale Politik Quarterly*, May 3, 2020. https://ip-quarterly.com/en/frances-welfare-state-kept-macron-power.

Lee Edwards, "The Myth of Scandinavian Socialism," the Heritage Foundation, April 20, 2022. https://www.heritage.org/progressivism/commentary/the-myth-scandinavian-socialism.

Stefan Hedlund, "Myths and Realities of the Nordic Welfare State," Geopolitical Intelligence Services, March 22, 2021. https://www.gisreportsonline.com/r/nordic-welfare-state/.

Yvette Lind, "Childcare Infrastructure in the Nordic Countries," Nordics Info, February 21, 2024. https://nordics.info/show/artikel/childcare-infrastructure-in-the-nordic-countries.

Dylan Matthews, "Denmark, Finland, and Sweden Are Proof That Poverty in the US Doesn't Have to Be This High," VOX, November 11, 2015. https://www.vox.com/policy-and-politics/2015/11/11/9707528/finland-poverty-united-states.

David McHugh, "Pandemic Shows Contrasts Between US, European Safety Nets," Associated Press, May 10, 2020. https://apnews.com/article/health-financial-markets-ap-top-news-financial-crisis-virus-outbreak-016b768f9c856c1baa1f7a6032de1243.

Emma Reynolds, "Europe's Social Safety Net is Often Considered the Gold Standard. Coronavirus Has Exposed Its Holes," CNN, December 6, 2020. https://www.cnn.com/2020/12/06/business/europe-covid-inequality-benefits-intl/index.html.

Chapter 4

What Is the Future of Welfare and Social Security?

Chapter Preface

The question of whether a government can effectively control its social safety net is a complex undertaking, and yet it is a challenge a government must meet for the health and wellbeing of its citizens. It's probably safe to say that most people would agree that such a system is vital whether they themselves have used their country's safety net, or if someone they personally know has done so. However, in the United States there are competing views on this subject.

Beyond considering what role the government should play in maintaining a social safety net today, many are concerned about whether it will be possible to maintain it in the future. Viewpoints in this chapter address many potential challenges for the future. Would the government be able to handle another global pandemic? Is the Social Security system broken, and can it be fixed? Should everyone benefit from safety net programs? People who are young today worry that the social safety net as we know it may cease to exist when they are ready for retirement, but some viewpoint authors argue that, with some effort, it will be possible to meet these challenges and ensure that social security programs persist.

The viewpoints in this chapter investigate these questions and create an understanding for readers of how these issues affect the future of welfare and social security programs.

VIEWPOINT 1

> "Where you have restrictions in place, where you have situations in which people cannot get to work, cannot do their jobs, at all or in the normal way, then clearly you have to have compensatory measures in place to support the income of working people, to support enterprises."

Countries Need to Be Better Prepared for Crises Like COVID

John Power

In the following viewpoint John Power asserts that countries need to have better social safety nets in place for crises like the COVID pandemic. Power argues that countries need to be ready to step in and support people in their jobs and other living situations in the midst of a crisis, and that the COVID pandemic showed that many countries are ill equipped to do this. In particular, he focuses on how countries in the Asia-Pacific region responded, but the claims he makes are true for many countries throughout the world. John Power is a journalist based in Melbourne, Australia, whose work has appeared in a number of media outlets.

"After COVID, Asia must bolster social safety net: UN labour chief," by John Power, Al Jazeera Media Network, January 21, 2022. Reprinted by permission.

What Is the Future of Welfare and Social Security?

As you read, consider the following questions:

1. According to this viewpoint, which global region needs to be better prepared for a crisis?
2. Which countries spend far below the average amount on social protection, as reported by Power?
3. Does the viewpoint predict that emerging economies will recover from the pandemic at the same level as developed countries?

Asia-Pacific countries should see the pandemic as a wake-up call to bolster their meagre social safety nets, the head of the U.N. labour agency has said.

In an exclusive interview with Al Jazeera, International Labour Organization (ILO) Director-General Guy Ryder said COVID-19 had revealed the need for "much more robust" social protection in the region, where border restrictions and business closures continue to inflict damage to livelihoods two years into the pandemic.

"The failure of some to do that or not to do so adequately, I think, has been part of the problem of dealing and having the necessary resilience to deal with the COVID pandemic," Ryder said.

Ryder added that while it was not his place to judge whether the public health responses of some countries were better than others, he believed the Asia-Pacific needed to better prepare itself for "future shocks" that could come from public health or other crises.

"Where you have restrictions in place, where you have situations in which people cannot get to work, cannot do their jobs, at all or in the normal way, then clearly you have to have compensatory measures in place to support the income of working people, to support enterprises," the UN labour agency chief said.

Many Asia-Pacific countries spend less than 2 percent of gross domestic product on social protection, excluding healthcare, according to a 2020 report by the ILO, far below the global average of 11 percent.

Welfare and Social Security Programs

Many Asia-Pacific countries have reported fewer deaths than their Western counterparts during the pandemic, but the region's ongoing border controls and business restrictions have inflicted heavy social and economic costs.

While the emergence of the Omicron variant has accelerated moves by some Western countries towards living with the virus—due to the variant's higher transmissibility and milder severity than previous strains—many Asia-Pacific economies have reversed or delayed steps towards reopening.

In recent weeks, economies including mainland China, Japan, Hong Kong, South Korea, Malaysia, and Singapore have tightened their borders. Mainland China, Hong Kong and South Korea have also reimposed domestic controls ranging from school closures to lockdowns and business curfews.

Despite high vaccination coverage, the Asia-Pacific was largely closed to travel even before the emergence of the new variant.

In October, travel in the region was down 92.8 percent compared with the same period in 2019, while air traffic in Europe and North America was down 51 percent and 57 percent, respectively.

Ryder said, however, he did believe the pandemic would not lead to a permanent unravelling of connectivity and globalisation in the Asia-Pacific.

"My view is we're not on the verge of stepping back from globalisation, we are not on a road to deglobalisation, nor would I wish to see these things, nor do I think they would be of benefit to any of the populations that I think we might consider," he said.

"I do not see not (sic) us being projected, if you like, along a trajectory of deglobalisation or retreat, not by virtue of the labour market impact of COVID on the world of work."

"Right Direction"

Ryder said that although the global economy was "moving in the right direction," he was concerned the pandemic recovery was both uncertain and unequal.

In its outlook for 2022 published earlier this week, the ILO predicted global employment would not recover to pre-pandemic levels until at least 2023. The U.N. agency projected the shortfall in hours worked this year would be equivalent to 52 million full-time jobs, a downgrade from previous forecasts, with underlying inequalities between countries "amplifying and prolonging the adverse impact of the crisis."

"While those in the higher income countries can look forward to levels of standards of living, levels of production that they knew pre-pandemic, it's not the case with developing countries, it's not the case with emerging economies," Ryder said.

VIEWPOINT 2

> "Welfare services—like unemployment benefits, health care and pensions—are how countries keep their populations healthy and productive in order to maintain robust and growing economies."

Social Welfare Services Must Be Maintained for the Good of the Country

Nehal El-Hadi and Daniel Merino

In the following viewpoint Nehal El-Hadi and Daniel Merino discuss the stresses placed on welfare systems and why services are being cut around the world. El-Hadi and Merino maintain that this is not sound policy and countries will suffer because of it. Cutting welfare leads to a rise in poverty, especially in the developing world, which then leads to a host of other issues. Nehal El-Hadi is the science and technology editor and co-host of the weekly podcast for the Conversation, and Daniel Merino is an associate science editor and co-host of the weekly podcast.

As you read, consider the following questions:

1. What do welfare systems protect countries against, according to the authors?

"Social welfare services are being cut across the world, but providing them is about more than just money – podcast," by Nehal El-Hadi and Daniel Merino, The Conversation, January 19, 2023. https://theconversation.com/social-welfare-services-are-being-cut-across-the-world-but-providing-them-is-about-more-than-just-money-podcast-198051. Licensed under CC-BY ND 4.0 International.

What Is the Future of Welfare and Social Security?

2. At the time this viewpoint was published in 2023, which countries were facing shutdowns of the welfare system?
3. What is the populist welfare state regime, according to El-Hadi and Merino?

Across the globe, health-care workers have gone on strike to protest the stress placed on them by the global COVID-19 pandemic and economic downturn, pushing already-strained services beyond their limits. These labour actions are part of the challenges faced by countries attempting to provide welfare services to their populations.

In this episode of *The Conversation Weekly* podcast, we talk to three experts about why social welfare services are being cut, and what actions governments may need to take to ensure better access.

Welfare services—like unemployment benefits, health care and pensions—are how countries keep their populations healthy and productive in order to maintain robust and growing economies.

Miguel Niño-Zarazúa is a senior lecturer in the Department of Economics at the School of Oriental and African Studies in London, U.K., who looks at welfare institutions in the global south. He explains that welfare systems are integrated social policies, which "have become one of the most important policy instruments against poverty and vulnerability in the developing world."

However, Niño-Zarazúa says that welfare institutions in developing nations are increasingly under threat. "In low-income countries in particular, now, we see many countries facing a debt crisis that has been accumulating over the last decade because they continue borrowing to sustain their economic growth."

But it's not just developing countries where access to welfare is diminishing. Christine Corlet Walker, who is a research fellow at the Centre for the Understanding of Sustainable Prosperity at the University of Surrey in the U.K. looks at member countries of the Organisation for Economic Co-operation and Development (OECD).

Welfare and Social Security Programs

Global economic growth is slowing down—and many experts expect it to approach zero or negative. Facing this, governments have responded with austerity measures and cuts to welfare services. "A post-growth welfare system is a welfare system that can function and can flourish in the absence of economic growth," Corlet Walker says, "and there's obviously a huge amount that can be done in terms of redistribution through progressive taxes on wealth and land, for example."

Erdem Yörük is an associate professor at Koç University in Istanbul in Turkey. He studies how developing countries implement welfare programs, but during his research, he found that existing scholarship on welfare excluded developing nations. "There are two reasons for this western or Eurocentrism," he explains. Scholars assume that "there is no welfare state because capitalism is not fully developed in the non-West as opposed to European countries.

Means Testing and the Future of Social Security

In 2015, the annual cost of Social Security retirement benefits equaled 14.1 percent of workers' taxable income. By 2038, it is projected that the cost will amount to 16.6 percent. Future Social Security tax revenues are projected to fall short of future benefit commitments.

The prospect of large, unpopular, tax increases or large, unpopular, benefit cuts has focused attention on using "means testing" to reduce Social Security payments for beneficiaries who are relatively well-off. Means testing can, however, be implemented in various ways, and as Alan Gustman, Thomas Steinmeier, and Nahid Tabatabai demonstrate in Distributional Effects of Means Testing Social Security: Income Versus Wealth (NBER Working Paper 22424), different approaches affect benefits for different households in different ways. The distributional consequences of means testing are sensitive to the way the means test is designed.

Means tests reduce payments for those with wealth or income above certain levels. The average Social Security benefit for an

What Is the Future of Welfare and Social Security?

The second reason, was that welfare systems regimes literature is a highly empirical literature. And so there was no data to conduct such similar analysis for the non-West."

So at first, Yörük and his team compiled the data. And he determined that there was an additional type of welfare regime beyond the three main types established by scholars of western countries, which he refers to as a "populist welfare state regime."

This type of regime uses the provision of welfare services as a political bargaining tool: this occurs during times of political unrest, as in Turkey where Yörük conducted his research, or to leverage the voting power of the poor during elections.

Because welfare services contribute to a productive society, it's imperative that governments understand the value of taking care of their populations. But during these uncertain economic times, countries are contending with the unprecedented and unexpected

---

individual in the top quarter of the income distribution was $16,400 in 2010. An income-based means test that reduced the average Social Security benefit for this group by $4,900 would reduce benefits by about 30 percent on average. The average reduction for those in the top quartile of the wealth distribution would be similar if the means test applied to wealth. Among the 14.5 percent of the individuals who are in both the top income and the top wealth quartiles, the average benefit reduction would be $8,600 if the test was applied to wealth.

The distributional consequences of means tests change if the unit of measurement changes from an individual to a household. They change if married households and single households are considered separately. They change if housing wealth is included. They depend upon whether a means test's measures of income and wealth are calculated before or after taxes. Means testing at program entry would reduce benefits more for younger retirees than older ones simply because younger people have not lived on their retirement resources for as many years.

"Means Testing Social Security: Income Versus Wealth," by Linda Gorman, National Bureau of Economic Research, September 2016.

expenditures produced by climate change mitigation, environmental disasters, the COVID-19 pandemic and political conflict.

Niño-Zarazúa believes that governments reduce access to social services at their own risk. "So despite the fact that many countries face substantial and very difficult challenges, there are always ways to finance and make savings or reorganize the spending to support these programs."

Cuts to welfare will only exacerbate the rates of poverty around the world. And as economic pressures increase on governments in both developed and developing nations, the provision of welfare is under risk. And the strain on welfare systems is felt not only by those attempting to access services, but also by those who work within them under these conditions.

VIEWPOINT 3

> *"Costs of the program are expected to further exceed the money that's coming in, which will continue to drain the trust fund, according to the program's trustees."*

The Future of Social Security Must Be Addressed Now

Andrew Rettenmaier and Dennis W. Jansen

In this viewpoint Andrew Rettenmaier and Dennis W. Jansen discuss the current state of the United States's Social Security program, which many people who are retired or have disabilities depend on to make ends meet. The program's trust fund is rapidly running out of money, and if it is drained—as the authors expect will happen soon—then there will be major cuts to Social Security benefits under the current law. The authors argue that this is an unacceptable outcome and one that can be addressed with certain political changes, but lawmakers must act now to prevent a catastrophe. Andrew Rettenmaier is the executive associate director of the Private Enterprise Research Center at Texas A&M University, where Dennis W. Jansen is a professor of economics and director of the Private Enterprise Research Center.

"Getting Social Security on a more stable path is hard but essential – 2 experts suggest a way forward," by Andrew Rettenmaier and Dennis W. Jansen, The Conversation, June 1, 2023, https://theconversation.com/getting-social-security-on-a-more-stable-path-is-hard-but-essential-2-experts-suggest-a-way-forward-206462. Licensed under CC BY-ND 4.0 International.

Welfare and Social Security Programs

As you read, consider the following questions:

1. According to the authors, when will the Social Security trust fund be drained?
2. How is Social Security funded, according to this viewpoint?
3. What was the last presidential administration to reform the Social Security program?

Social Security is in trouble.
The retirement and disability program has been running a cash-flow deficit since 2010. Its trust fund, which holds US$2.7 trillion, is rapidly diminishing. Social Security's trustees, a group that includes the secretaries of the departments of Treasury, Labor, and Health and Human Services, as well as the Social Security commissioner, project that the trust fund will be completely drained by 2033.

Under current law, when that trust fund is empty, Social Security can pay benefits only from dedicated tax revenues, which would by that point cover about 77% of promised benefits. Another way to say this is that when the trust fund is depleted, under current law, Social Security beneficiaries would see a sudden 23% cut in their monthly checks in 2034.

As economists who study the Medicare and Social Security programs, we view the above scenario as politically unacceptable. Such a sudden and dramatic benefit cut would anger a lot of voters. Unfortunately, the actions necessary now to avoid it—like raising taxes or cutting benefits—aren't getting serious consideration today. But we believe there are strategies that could work.

Where the Money for Benefits Comes From

Roughly 67 million Americans, most of whom are 65 or older, receive Social Security benefits. The agency disburses more than $1 trillion annually. It's the government's largest single expenditure, constituting nearly 20% of the total federal budget.

Social Security is funded by a payroll tax of 12.4% on wages split equally between workers and employers. Self-employed people pay the entire 12.4%. This payroll tax applies to earnings up to $160,200 as of 2023. The government increases this cap annually based on increases in the National Average Wage Index—a measure that combines wage growth and inflation. The program also receives about 4% of its revenue from a tax on Social Security benefits, though not everyone who receives them has to pay this tax.

Social Security tax revenue stayed relatively flat after 1990. But the costs of the program rose sharply in 2010, in part because of early retirements in response to the Great Recession.

Social Security spending has recently been growing more rapidly because of a wave of baby boomer retirements, which added to a decline in the number of workers per retiree.

Costs of the program are expected to further exceed the money that's coming in, which will continue to drain the trust fund, according to the program's trustees.

Barring immediate action by the government, the trust fund's exhaustion is only a little more than a decade away. And yet few members of Congress seem willing to do something about it. For example, Social Security reform was not even on the table during the 2023 negotiations over the debt ceiling and spending cuts.

Trust Fund

Where did the trust fund, which helps cover the program's costs, come from?

While the Social Security program was collecting surpluses from 1984 to 2009, that extra money funded other spending—keeping other taxes lower than they would have been otherwise and partially covering the budget deficit.

During Social Security's years of surplus, the excess revenues were credited to the trust fund in the form of special-issue government bonds that yielded the prevailing interest rates. When those bonds are needed to pay for Social Security expenses, the Treasury redeems them.

Those bonds are components of the government's $31.4 trillion gross debt.

Last Reformed During the Reagan Administration

Reducing the benefits current retirees receive would be extremely unpopular. Likewise, people now in the workforce who are nearing retirement would certainly object strongly if they were told to expect lower benefits in retirement than they have been promised throughout their careers.

The last time the government made big changes to Social Security was in 1983, during the Reagan administration, when the government enacted reforms that slowly reduced benefits over time. These changes included raising the full retirement age, a change that is still being phased in. Because of those changes, workers born in 1960 or later cannot retire with full benefits until age 67—two years later than the original retirement age.

The 1983 reforms also included increases in the Social Security payroll tax rate from 10.4% in 1983 to 12.4% by 1990, and for the first time levied federal income taxes on higher-income retirees' benefits. Workers bore the burden of the payroll tax increases and higher-income retirees bore the burden of the tax on benefits.

Those changes bolstered the program's finances, but they no longer suffice.

The bipartisan 2001 Commission to Strengthen Social Security tried—and failed—during George W. Bush's presidency to get Congress to enact reforms to shore up the program's finances. There's been no momentum toward resolving the problem since then.

Four Principles

We believe that policymakers and lawmakers need to follow four principles as they consider how to move forward.

1. The program should be self-funded in the long run so that its annual revenues match its annual expenses. That way the many questions that arise related to trust fund accounting and whether Social Security tax revenues are being used for their intended purposes would be eliminated.
2. The reform burden should be shared across generations. Current retirees can share the burden through a reform that reduces the cost-of-living adjustment. Today's workers can share the burden through an increase in the cap on income subjected to Social Security taxes so that 90% of total earnings are taxed. Continued gradual increases in the retirement age to keep pace with anticipated longevity gains would also be borne by current workers.
3. The government should make sure that Social Security benefits will be adequate for lower-income retirees for years to come. That means reforms that slow the benefit growth of future retirees would be designed to affect only higher-income retirees.
4. Any changes to Social Security should help constrain the future growth of federal spending, given the current and projected growth in the budget deficit.

Advantages of Ending the Delay

It appears that the United States—citizens and elected officials included—are deferring serious debate on this urgent matter until the trust fund's depletion is imminent. That's unwise. Acting sooner rather than later would leave more options available to gradually resolve the program's financial shortfalls.

Ending this procrastination would also give the millions of people who rely on Social Security benefits, taxpayers and businesses more time to prepare for any changes required by overdue reforms.

VIEWPOINT 4

> "There is widespread agreement among experts that high inequality destabilises societies. Increasing inequality can undermine democracy, trust between social groups and institutions, and even result in substantial changes to the political order."

Welfare Can Pave the Way to More Equal Societies and Less Conflict

Patricia Justino

In this viewpoint, which was originally published in early 2020, Patricia Justino asserts that reducing inequality through the use of welfare offers many positive benefits to society. Conversely, inequality creates social tensions and has a detrimental impact on economic growth. Justino argues that income inequality is behind many political demonstrations around the world as well as a factor that has destabilized many democracies. In order to ensure a more stable social and political future, welfare programs must be protected and strengthened. Patricia Justino is a development economist and deputy director of the United Nations University World Institute for Development Economics Research.

"Welfare works: redistribution is the way to create less violent, less unequal societies," by Patricia Justino, The Conversation, March 12, 2020, https://theconversation.com/welfare-works-redistribution-is-the-way-to-create-less-violent-less-unequal-societies-128807. Licensed under CC BY-ND 4.0 International.

Welfare and Social Security Programs

As you read, consider the following questions:

1. What does Justino argue is behind the increase in inequality that has occurred since the 1980s?
2. According to this viewpoint, why does inequality lower economic growth?
3. According to Justino, how does the United States's tolerance for inequality compare to other countries? What does she consider as evidence of this?

In his presidential address to the Royal Economic Society in 1996, the late professor Anthony Atkinson famously called for discussion of inequality and income distribution to be brought "in from the cold." Since then there have been many examples of inequality worldwide: the pan-banging *cacerolazos* demonstrators of Argentina's financial crisis in 2001-2002, the Arab Spring, the Occupy Wall Street movement, Spain's "los indignados," the "gilets jaunes" protests and strikes in France, and many others besides.

It was almost 20 years before the subject became a matter of mainstream debate, perhaps signified by the publication and success of Thomas Piketty's *Capital* in 2014. Yet the statistics that show rising inequality are well-known and have been staring us in the face for decades. In the United States, the top 1% of the population accounts for 20% of total national income and more than 30% of wealth. Worldwide, around 9% of the population receives 50% of global income, while the bottom half the world's population receive a mere 7%.

This inequality has been increasing since the 1980s when a series of social, economic, and political factors—including a shift of employment from factories and manufacturing into services and more differentiated jobs, the weakening of trade unions, more wage competition facilitated by globalisation, and fiscal pressures on welfare systems—combined to sustain rises in inequality not seen since the 1920s.

It is now known that inequality lowers economic growth by reducing middle-class demand and increasing the costs of redistribution. It causes poverty traps by reducing social mobility, and creates social tensions.

The "trickle-down economics" ideology that dominated the 1980s and 1990s (and which has now reappeared in US president Donald Trump's tax plan) has been well and truly debunked: economic growth does not automatically produce better lives for everyone.

There is widespread agreement among experts that high inequality destabilises societies. Increasing inequality can undermine democracy, trust between social groups and institutions, and even result in substantial changes to the political order. Today, increases in inequality have been accompanied by unprecedented growth of far-right politics, growing protest movements, and the election of governments with nationalistic overtones.

There are steps that could be taken to curtail rising inequality, but not a great deal is being done.

What Works

In research drawn from 18 countries across Latin America between 2010 and 2014, we found that those taking part in protests were more likely to be strongly in favour of redistribution, and were motivated by the perceived failure of public services, institutions, corruption and lower standards of living. But some countries—the United States, for example—are tolerant of inequality, as can be seen for example in how the United States has a less progressive tax system, less public spending to benefit the poorer off, and limited employment rights in comparison to European countries.

When inequality reaches certain thresholds, it may lead to social conflict and sometimes violence. Whether or not it gets to this stage depends on whether action is taken to reduce inequality. One solution to avoid potential instability is to redistribute wealth through welfare programmes.

About half the reduction in violent conflict experienced in Latin America since the 1990s can be attributed to increases in government welfare spending, largely in the form of cash transfer programmes. Welfare transfers are also an effective (and cheaper) means to mitigating riots than the police—as can be seen looking at data from India between 1960-2011 where states with higher levels of welfare spending experienced less rioting.

The relationship between welfare programmes and socio-political tensions has deep historical roots. Otto von Bismarck initiated the world's first social insurance programme when he was chancellor of Germany in the late 19th century as a response to the threat of social instability by dissatisfied workers' unions. The idea of using welfare transfers to curtail potential instability spread rapidly across Europe during the early 20th century, becoming a central part of a social contract between states and citizens.

But welfare spending has been drastically reduced across the world since the 1980s, and it may not be surprising that inequality and social tensions have risen at the same time.

Welfare policies, such as cash transfers to the poor, unemployment benefits, child subsidies and universal health care—funded by progressive taxation—can break cycles of poverty and social discontent by addressing economic vulnerabilities and reinforcing resilience among those least well-off. More fundamentally, today, as in Europe at the turn of the 20th century, welfare programmes can sustain peace and stability because they remain a central part of the social contract between states and citizens.

When the social contract is seen to be broken, those that lose out feel disenfranchised and at the margin of societies while a few continue to amass great fortunes at the cost of the many. But unchecked rises in inequality come at a high societal cost, from protests and strikes, to the rise of nationalism and autocracy. It may well be high time to bring redistribution in from the cold.

Welfare and Social Security Programs

Periodical and Internet Sources Bibliography

The following articles have been selected to supplement the diverse views presented in this chapter.

Henry J. Aaron and Katherine Baicker, "Is the Safety Net Ready for the Next Public Health Emergency?" Brookings, July 26, 2023. https://www.brookings.edu/articles/is-the-safety-net-ready-for-the-next-public-health-emergency/.

Laura Combs, "The Future of Social Security and Medicare," Mercer Advisors, September 11, 2023. https://www.merceradvisors.com/insights/retirement/the-future-of-social-security-and-medicare/.

Alexandra C. Gaines, Bradley Hardy, and Justin Schweitzer, "How Weak Safety Net Policies Exacerbate Regional and Racial Inequality," the Center for American Progress, September 22, 2021. https://www.americanprogress.org/article/weak-safety-net-policies-exacerbate-regional-racial-inequality/.

Ayurella Horn-Muller, "The Hidden Hurdles of Social Safety Net Programs," Axios, March 29, 2023. https://www.axios.com/2023/03/29/social-safety-net-hurdles.

Jeffrey M. Jones, "Americans More Upbeat About Future Social Security Benefits," Gallup, December 8, 2023, https://news.gallup.com/poll/546890/americans-upbeat-future-social-security-benefits.aspx.

Lorie Konish, "Social Security's Trust Funds May Run Out in 2034. These Changes May Help," CNBC, November 8, 2023. https://www.cnbc.com/2023/11/08/these-changes-may-fix-social-security-before-2034-benefit-shortfall.html.

Cora Lewis, "How Social Security Works and What to Know About Its Future," Associated Press, October 13, 2022. https://apnews.com/article/how-does-social-security-work-91e2d237d93e2ac7d2775e8b19d2a7a1.

Robert A. Moffitt and James P. Ziliak, "Making the U.S. Safety Net More Responsive to Economic Downturns," Institute for Research on Poverty, April 2021. https://www.irp.wisc.edu/resource/making-the-u-s-safety-net-more-responsive-to-economic-downturns/.

Trina Paul, "Will Social Security Run Out of Money? Here's What Could Happen to Your Benefits If Congress Doesn't Act," CNBC, July 30, 2023. https://www.cnbc.com/select/will-social-security-run-out-heres-what-you-need-to-know/.

Amanda Renteria and Tracey Patterson, "Our Path Forward to Transform the Social Safety Net," Code for America, April 12, 2022. https://codeforamerica.org/news/our-path-forward-to-transform-the-social-safety-net/.

John Waggoner, "9 Ways to Strengthen Social Security," AARP, April 11, 2023. https://www.aarp.org/retirement/social-security/info-2022/benefits-current-status-future-stability.html.

For Further Discussion

Chapter 1
1. Based on what you've read in the viewpoints in this chapter, is government spending on social security programs valuable? What programs in particular are valuable?
2. According to the viewpoints in this chapter, how have the welfare system and social security programs changed over time?
3. Based on what you've read in the viewpoint by Alma Carten and other viewpoints, what impact does racism have on federal assistance programs?

Chapter 2
1. Does political affiliation have an impact on beliefs about government spending and assistance programs? Use evidence from viewpoints in this chapter to support your conclusions.
2. Should the government be responsible for helping lift people out of poverty? Use specific details from the viewpoints in this chapter to support your argument.
3. There is a common argument that many people take advantage of the welfare system and social security programs. Using evidence from viewpoints in this chapter, does this seem to be a common issue? Why or why not?

Chapter 3
1. A number of viewpoints in this chapter indicate that the United States has a poor health care system compared to other developed nations. What reasons do the viewpoints in this chapter offer for this?
2. Why do some countries have better social welfare systems than others?

3. Based on what you've read in the viewpoints in this chapter, what indicates that a country has effective social welfare and health care systems?

Chapter 4

1. According to the viewpoints in this chapter, what are some current challenges to welfare and social security programs around the world? How might these impact the future of these programs?
2. According to the viewpoints in this chapter, cuts to welfare and social safety net programs will increase poverty and instability around the world. Do past and current events back up this claim? Use facts from viewpoints in this volume to back up your argument.
3. What suggestions do the authors in this chapter offer for how to improve welfare and social security programs and ensure they are able to continue?

Organizations to Contact

The editors have compiled the following list of organizations concerned with the issues debated in this book. The descriptions are derived from materials provided by the organizations. All have publications or information available for interested readers. The list was compiled on the date of publication of the present volume; the information provided here may change. Be aware that many organizations take several weeks or longer to respond to inquiries, so allow as much time as possible.

Center for American Progress (CAP)

1333 H Street, NW, Suite 100E
Washington, DC 20005
(202) 682-1611
website: www.americanprogress.org

The Center for American Progress is an independent, progressive, nonpartisan organization dedicated to improving the lives of all Americans. It aims to implement big ideas on climate change, gun control, pay equity, social safety nets, and more.

Center on Budget and Policy Priorities (CBPP)

1275 First Street NE, Suite 1200
Washington, DC 20002
(202) 408-1080
email: info@cbpp.org
website: www.cbpp.org

The CBPP is a nonpartisan research and policy agency. Its mission is to advance legislation and policies to create a nation where everyone has the appropriate resources to share and thrive in the United States.

Code for America

972 Mission St, 5th Floor
San Francisco, CA 94103
(415) 816-1286
website: https://codeforamerica.org

Code for America is a charitable organization that has a vision to influence the government to construct an equitable and resilient social safety net. It wants to have a safety net that is human-centered, and one that is simple to use and easy to access.

Habitat for Humanity

285 Peachtree Center Ave NE Suite 2700
Atlanta, GA 30303
(800) 422-4828
website: www.habitat.org

Habitat for Humanity is an organization that helps homeowners build their own homes at an affordable cost. The organization partners with people in many communities and around the world. It gives homeowners the chance to have stability and independence in their lives and a better place to live for themselves and their families.

Hoover Institution

1399 New York Ave. NW, Suite 500
Washington, DC 20005
website: www.hoover.org

The Hoover Institution is a public policy think tank. The organization promotes economic prosperity and opportunity for all, and consequently it is active in securing an equitable social safety net for the present and the future.

Welfare and Social Security Programs

Human Rights Watch

350 Fifth Ave, 34th floor
New York, NY 10118
(212) 290-4700
website: www.hrw.org

Human Rights Watch is an organization that works to protect the rights of many groups of people. It advocates for and helps the disabled, elderly, women, children, minorities, LGBTQIA+ persons, and many others.

Medicaid.gov

7500 Security Boulevard
Baltimore, MD 21244
Phone: (800) 877-8339
email: Medicaid.gov@cms.hhs.gov
website: www.medicaid.gov

Medicaid.gov offers information on the Medicaid program, CHIP services, and the Basic Health Program. These are health safety net programs that provide health coverage for children, pregnant women, families, adults without children, seniors, and people with disabilities. The website offers guidance on what these programs cover and how to request assistance.

Social Security Administration (SSA)

1100 West High Rise, 6401 Security Blvd.
Baltimore, MD 21235
(800) 772-1213
website: www.ssa.gov

The Social Security Administration is a governmental agency of the United States. The SSA is a major player in the social safety net of the United States. Millions of Americans receive benefits from this agency. Benefits include retirement assistance for seniors and social services for those who are disabled and others unable to work.

USAGov

(844) 872-4681
website: www.usa.gov

USAGov is the official guide to government services and information in the United States. Find out about any of the social services that could be of help to you and your family through this website.

U. S. Department of Health and Human Services

200 Independence Ave, SW
Washington, DC 20201
(877) 696-6775
website: www.hhs.gov

The U.S. Department of Health and Human Services is a government agency of the United States. Its mission is to enhance the health and wellbeing of all Americans. This agency maintains a website with a wealth of information about social services for families, children, and individuals.

Bibliography of Books

Nancy J. Altman and Eric Kingson. *Social Security Works for Everyone! Protecting and Expanding the Insurance Americans Love and Count On.* New York, NY: The New Press, 2021.

Marcia Amidon Lüsted. *Universal Health Care* (At Issue). New York, NY: Greenhaven Publishing, 2019.

Courtney C. Coile, Kevin Milligan, and David A. Wise, eds. *Social Security Programs and Retirement Around the World* (National Bureau of Economic Research Conference Report). Chicago, IL: University of Chicago Press, 2019.

M. M. Eboch. *Income Inequality* (Introducing Issues with Opposing Viewpoints). New York, NY: Greenhaven Publishing, 2022.

M. M. Eboch. *Universal Basic Income* (Introducing Issues with Opposing Viewpoints). New York, NY: Greenhaven Publishing, 2022.

Kathryn J. Edin, H. Luke Shaefer, and Timothy J. Nelson. *The Injustice of Place: Uncovering the Legacy of Poverty in America.* New York, NY: Mariner Books, 2023.

Kristina Lyn Heitkamp. *Learned Helplessness, Welfare, and the Poverty Cycle* (Current Controversies). New York, NY: Greenhaven Publishing, 2019.

Joanne Goldblum and Colleen Shaddox. *Broke in America: Seeing, Understanding, and Ending U.S. Poverty.* Dallas, TX: BenBella Books, 2021.

Christopher Howard. *Who Cares: The Social Safety Net in America.* New York, NY: Oxford University Press, 2023.

Katarina Jovanovic. *Cardboard City.* Vancouver, BC: Tradewind Books, 2023.

Morlock, Rachael. *The Poverty Problem* (Spotlight on Global Issues). New York, NY: Rosen Publishing, 2022.

Lincoln Rice. *The Ethics of Protection: Reimagining Child Welfare in an Anti-Black Society.* Minneapolis, MN: Fortress Press, 2023.

David Wagner. *Poverty and Welfare in America: Examining the Facts* (Contemporary Debates). Santa Barbara, CA: ABC-CLIO, 2019.

Index

A

abuse of system, 15, 19–22, 58, 64–71, 83–96
after-school program, 91, 94
Aid to Families of Dependent Children, 44–48, 86
American Enterprise Institute, 39–42
American Medical Association, 25
Anderson, Bob, 90–92
Anderson, Chloe, 125–135
Arab Spring, 156
Area Redevelopment Act, 36
Argentina, 156
Atkinson, Anthony, 156
Australia, 113–114, 121, 125–135

B

Bachelet, Michelle, 109
Baird, Sarah Jane, 70
Bialik, 59–63
Biden, Joe, 39–42
Bismarck, Otto von, 158
Bolivia, 108
Bryan, Hob, 95
Bryant, Phil, 92
Bush, George W., 152

C

Cabo Verde, 108

Callaghan, Timothy, 119–124
Canada, 113–114, 121, 125–135
Carter, Alma, 43–54
Center for American Progress, 19–28
child care, 27, 41, 91, 95–96, 114
children, 15, 22, 25, 27, 30, 37, 39–48, 60, 67, 91–93, 95, 108–109, 120, 122, 130, 158
China, 142
civil rights, 24
Clinton, Bill, 15, 39–40, 44, 47, 65
Clinton, Hillary, 120
Commonwealth Fund, 113, 122, 126, 129, 131
Congress (U.S.), 23, 25, 29–30, 32, 36–38, 40, 46–47, 63, 73, 95, 124, 151–152
Congressional Budget Office, 41
Contract with America, 47
Corlet Walker, Christine, 145–146
cost of public benefits, 21, 37–38, 40, 46, 146
COVID-19, 39, 41, 140–143, 145, 148

D

Davis, John, 92
Demby, Gene, 83–87
Democratic Party, 59, 61–63, 73, 77, 79–81, 89
Denmark, 125–135

Index

De Witte, Melissa, 97–102
disability, 15, 18, 21–23, 26, 42, 53, 58, 60, 108–109, 127, 130
discrimination, 26, 43–46
Doar, Robert, 41
drug testing, 91

E

Economic Opportunity Act (1964), 24, 29–38
economy, 28, 32, 37, 40, 43, 70, 131–132, 145–148, 155–159
education assistance, 23–25, 29–34, 36–37, 53, 67–69, 94, 114, 116, 122
  Elementary and Secondary Education Act, 25
  Head Start, 25, 53
  Higher Education Act (1965), 25
  student loans, 25, 27, 76
  work-study, 33–34
elderly, 14–15, 18, 20–21, 23, 25, 34, 36, 45, 60, 75, 77–78, 108–109, 122–123, 144–145, 151
El-Hadi, Nehal, 144–148
Ellwood, David, 48
energy assistance, 23, 27, 50, 52
entitlement, 22–24, 27, 73, 76–80, 119, 123
environment, 24, 109, 148

F

Family First Prevention Services Act, 91
Fessler, Pam, 50–54

Flynn, Frank, 99
food assistance, 26–27, 32, 36, 39, 41–42, 47–48, 50, 52, 65, 68–69, 73, 75–77, 81, 116, 122, 127
  school lunch, 53
  Supplemental Nutrition Assistance Program, 15, 22–23
France, 114, 121, 125–135, 156

G

gender, 74, 80
Germany, 114, 121, 125–135, 158
gig economy, 109
Gingrich, Newt, 47
Global Partnership for Universal Social Protection, 108, 110
Good, Kayla, 98
government spending, 18, 22–27, 34–35, 37, 40, 42, 75, 89, 122–123, 126–128, 130–135, 141, 150–151, 158
government responsibility, 18, 25, 37, 57–103, 106, 121, 124, 139
Great Depression, 14
Great Recession, 22, 151
Greenfield, Deborah, 108
Gustman, Alan, 146

H

Hanna, Rema, 64–71
health care assistance, 27, 36, 41, 53, 108, 112–135, 141, 144–145
  Affordable Care Act, 60–61, 63, 119–120, 123, 126–127

171

Welfare and Social Security Programs

Medicaid, 22–23, 25, 47–48, 59–63, 65, 73, 75–77, 81, 120–121, 128
Medicare, 19–21, 23, 25, 59, 62–63, 73–79, 128, 150
Medicare and Medicaid Act (1965), 25
universal coverage, 114, 119–124, 158
Health, Education, and Welfare Department (U.S.), 34
Hong Kong, 142
housing assistance, 23, 27, 42, 116, 122, 127, 130
homelessness, 47, 52
Housing and Urban Development Act (1965), 24
Human Rights Watch, 14

I

illness, 15, 31, 58
immigration, 36, 48, 80, 121
income inequality, 155–159
India, 158
Indonesia, 64–71
infrastructure, 24, 50–51, 95, 116
injury, 15, 53, 108
Institute of Medicine, 131
International Federation of Health Plans, 129
International Labor Organization, 106–111, 141, 143

J

Jansen, Dennis W., 149–154

Japan, 121, 125–135, 142
Jim Crow laws, 45
Job Corps, 33
job creation, 31, 34
Johnson, Lyndon B., 15, 24–25, 29–38, 50–52
Justino, Patricia, 155–159

K

Kennedy, John F., 24, 45

L

Labor Department (U.S.), 33
Lesotho, 108
Levin, Josh, 84–87

M

Malaysia, 142
Manpower Development Training Act, 36
Markus, Hazel, 101
marriage, 15
maternity benefits, 108, 115, 122
McKenzie, David J., 70
Merino, Daniel, 144–148
Miller, Dale, 99
minimum wage, 36
Mississippi Child Protection Services, 91, 93
Mississippi Children's Home Society, 94
Mississippi Department of Education, 94

Index

Mississippi Department of Human Services, 89–94
Mongolia, 108
Morin, Rich, 72–82
Moses, Joy, 19–28
Moynihan, Daniel, 40

N

Namibia, 108
national debt, 47, 145
natural disaster, 58, 148
Netherlands, 114, 125–135
New Deal, 25, 44
New Federalism, 46
New, Nancy, 94
New Summit (school), 94
New Zealand, 114, 125–135
Niño-Zarazúa, Miguel, 145, 148
Nixon, Richard M., 15, 46
Norway, 114–115, 125–135

O

Obama, Barack, 48, 73, 77, 120
Occupy Wall Street, 156
Office of Economic Opportunity, 33, 35–36
Organization for Economic Cooperation and Development, 109–110, 122, 126–135, 145
Ortiz, Isabel, 110
Özler, Berk, 70

P

Patten, Eileen, 72–82
Pelosi, Nancy, 40
Personal Responsibility and Work Opportunity Reconciliation Act, 44
Piketty, Thomas, 156
Power, John, 140–143

R

race/ethnicity, 18, 24, 31, 43–54, 62, 74–76, 79–80, 84–85, 106, 131
Rachidi, Angela, 42
Ramos, Gabriela, 110
Reagan, Ronald, 42–43, 46–47, 84, 152
Recovery Act, 22
Reeves, Tate, 89, 92
refusal of assistance, 15
Republican Party, 23, 40, 47–48, 59, 61–63, 73, 77, 79–81, 88–90
retirement, 15, 21, 26, 35, 45, 130, 147, 151–153
Rettenmaier, Andrew, 149–154
Romney, Mitt, 73, 77
Roosevelt, Franklin D., 14, 44, 46
Rutkowski, Michal, 109
Ryder, Guy, 141–142

S

Sanders, Bernie, 121
Schneider, Eric C., 112–118
Schnurer, Eric, 85–86
Scott, Omeria, 90
Shriver, Sargent, 36
sick leave, 114

Singapore, 142
small business loans, 29
Social Security, 15, 18–23, 26, 48, 50, 52, 54, 73–79, 81, 139, 146–147, 149–154
  legislation, 14, 44–45, 61
South Africa, 108
South Korea, 142
Spain, 156
Squires, David, 125–135
Stanford SPARQ, 98, 101
states' responsibility, 40, 46
Steinmeier, Thomas, 146
stock market, 14, 21
Supreme Court (U.S.), 45
Sweden, 114, 121, 125–135
Switzerland, 114–115, 125–135

T

Tabatabai, Nahid, 146
taxes, 18–19, 21, 27, 31, 39, 41–42, 45, 47, 106, 110, 128, 146, 150–154, 157–158
Taylor, Linda, 83–87
Taylor, Paul, 72–82
Temporary Assistance for Needy Families, 22, 48, 65, 88, 90–95
Tikkanen, Roosa, 122
Timor Leste, 108
Trump, Donald, 63, 65, 120

U

unemployment insurance, 15, 19–21, 24–27, 29, 35–36, 42, 50, 53, 60, 73, 75–76, 81, 114, 122, 130, 144–145, 158
United Kingdom, 113–114, 121, 125–135
United Nations, 44, 109, 141, 143
universal social protection, 108–111
urban renewal, 24

V

veteran benefits, 76
Vocational Education Act, 36

W

Weidinger, Matt, 39–42
welfare reform, 39–44, 46–47, 95, 150–153
Wolfe, Anna, 88–96
work requirement, 48, 65
World Bank, 66, 70, 109

Y

Yörük, Erdem, 146–147

Z

Zaki, Jamil, 99
Zhao, Xuan, 97–102

Index

Welfare and Social Security Programs